SOUTH SEA STORIES

Tales from Papua New Guinea

SOUTH SEA STORIES

Tales from Papua New Guinea

Christopher Somerville

illustrated by the author

Published by
the Paperback Division of
W.H. ALLEN & Co. PLC.

A Target Book
Published in 1985
by the Paperback Division of
W. H. Allen & Co. PLC
44 Hill Street, London W1X 8LB

Printed in Great Britain by
Cox & Wyman Ltd, Reading

ISBN 0 426 20180 9

Contents

JOSEPH NIMA WALKS TO SCHOOL

THE ROAD SNAKES AWAY down the valley, dusty and full of stones. In the gloom of early morning, the thick jungle each side looks like a dark blanket stretching up to the feet of the high jagged mountains that encircle the valley. The first green fingers of light show the mountain tops up as a crooked, unbroken line in every direction. The sun has not yet hauled itself up above their shaggy heads to peer down on the pandanus trees and the rough road.

It is very quiet. Only a light rustling breaks the silence as the breeze trembles the millions of leaves and grasses in the forest.

The road crosses a wide, fast-flowing river on a rickety wood-and-tin bridge eighty feet above the water. On the hand-rail of the bridge perches a small bird with a long feathery tail. He looks drab and ordinary as he rocks gently to and fro in the half light, tapping his beak on the wooden rail. But if the sun were up, you would marvel at his colours — blue, green, chestnut, midnight black, snowy white and peach.

The bird suddenly cocks up his head and sits very still. Some noise not of water or wind has alarmed him. His bright black eyes stare sideways, unblinking, as he listens. A stone clicks and rolls along the road a hundred yards away. With a chakker of warning the Bird of Paradise jumps off the bridge rail, and flutters away over the grass and into the protective shade of the forest.

A boy of about ten comes down the road between the two dark blankets of jungle. His bare, hard-skinned feet raise little puffs of dry dust as he walks. A string bag of books dangles from one hand, and a large green leaf clutched under his arm holds two cold boiled sweet potatoes. He is dressed in a short-sleeved check shirt two sizes too big for him, and a pair of well-washed khaki shorts. A pencil is pushed into his tight, curly brown hair.

He stops on the bridge, puts down his books and leaf bundle, and reaches into his shirt pocket for a pebble. He draws back a brown-skinned arm and throws the pebble high and far, watching it skimming pandanus leaves and plummeting down with a splash into the steaming cold river. The boy picks up the bag and bundle and walks on, yawning and shivering and looking for the rim of the rising sun above the mountains.

The boy is Joseph Nima, on his daily five-mile walk from Kopi village in the hills to the mission school in the Wahgi Valley. His clan, the Kopi Nokpa people, have lived in the same place for thousands of years — for ever, Joseph thinks. They are members of only one of the hundreds of tribes that live in the mountains and on the coast of the long, dinosaur-shaped island of Papua New Guinea.

Joseph is the first member of his family to go to school. There he is learning about the world outside the Wahgi Valley — about Australia, the country of his teacher, Brother Tim, far away to the South across the sea; about the other tribes and peoples of Papua New Guinea, and the way they live. In class he sits next to Michael Tipuka, of the Neno tribe. Twenty years ago, their fathers fought on opposite sides with spears and bows and arrows in a great tribal battle on the spot where the mission school now stands. With a well-aimed arrow Michael's father actually gave the father of Joseph the white scar that he still carries on his stomach. Today their sons will play marbles together and copy each other's answers.

At school each day, Joseph is a boy of the modern world. But at home in Kopi village every evening, tired out from the long hike up the dusty Highlands Highway, he sits by the warm red glow of the fire, full of sweet potato and fish, chin on his knees and eyes half closed against the yellow smoke, to listen to the old stories of his tribe as they are told with laughter and many interruptions.

Joseph's mother, Jipona, likes to sing to Piau the baby, crooning her to sleep; and Rima, his father, tells funny stories when the wide bamboo tubes of strong black tobacco are passed around the fire, and the caps pop off the beer bottles. But for skill in telling the ancient, well-loved tales, handed on from generation to generation across uncounted years, there is no-one who can touch his grandfather, Kian Kombuk. The old man sits cross-legged near the hot fire-stones, rolling tobacco in a half sheet torn from a newspaper with his blunt fingers, twisted from work.

"Come on, Kian — how about 'Sigal and Migal' tonight?" suggests someone, and other voices take up the plea.

"Yes, let's hear that one, Kian — how does it start?"

Everyone knows that the old man loves to tell a

story, but won't be hurried into it. He looks around the circle of fire-lit faces as he picks up a live coal in his horny hand to light his long, bent cigarette. Kian makes them wait, inhaling several lungfuls of acrid smoke and scratching his white beard as he pretends to search his memory for the words he must have spoken a thousand times.

"How many stories do you know, grandfather?" Joseph asked one day as they sat in the shade of the pandanus tree that grew beside the house. Old Kian grinned at his small grandson and pointed up into the green foliage above them. Dark clusters of pandanus nuts hung among the leaves.

"How many? As many as that . . . and one more," chuckled the old man.

Most nights Kian Kombuk tells a story, digging back into the hoard of legends that lie locked in his grizzled head. Rima works as he listens, smoothing off an axe-handle with his one-dollar knife, a green stumpy bottle of "South Pacific" beer between his knees. Jipona croons under her breath, rocking the baby in the crook of her arm. Joseph's aunts chew betel nuts, spitting the bright red juice into the fire, occasionally refreshing their mouths with a bite of lime leaf. On the woven bamboo walls, spiders with luminous green knees and feet scuttle after flies, and bush rats rustle in the sooty thatch overhead. Joseph's half-open eyes stare dreamily out of the low doorway at a patch of starry sky. The growl of Kian's voice, telling the tale of Sigal and Migal, is mixed up with his own thoughts.

" . . . so they put some taros into their string bags, and set off from the village . . . "

Brother Tim was in a bad mood today; the plane from Goroka hasn't been able to land because of the clouds. He'll have to wait another whole week for those new seeds for the food gardens.

" . . . but when Sigal tried to get up again, she was stuck fast to the rock . . . "

Jipona has put two sweetcorns in his bag for tomorrow. Maybe Pius Umbu will swap his mouth harp for one of them.

" . . . the parents waited all night, but there was no sign of Sigal or Migal . . . "

Is there really a crocodile in the Wahgi River, swum up from the sea with small boys on his menu, as Rima has told him? His father is probably just having one of his jokes, but it's not always easy to tell.

" . . . they pulled and pulled, but Sigal and Migal were stuck tight and could not be moved . . . "

The fire is too hot tonight. He can feel the skin burning on his left side. If only he were not feeling so sleepy, he would roll further away . . .

" . . . and that part of the bush is still called Sigalmigal. You can still see the two sisters sitting on their rock, stiff as stones among the trees."

Kian Kombuk finishes his story. Piau is asleep in the crook of Jipona's arm, and Jipona can see Joseph's head sagging towards the earth floor. The listeners yawn, stand up and stretch, scratching their scalps. They shake the hands of Rima and the old man, and go slowly out and across the village square to their own houses.

Joseph curls up on his mat, and pulls the thick grey trade-store blanket up around his ears. Highland nights are chilly. Kian finishes his smoke by the fire and lies down in his place. A shower of rain patters across the village, hissing on the grass roofs and drenching the sugar-canes in the gardens beyond the pig-fence, but no-one is awake to hear it.

HOW FIRE CAME TO THE HIGHLANDS

JIPONA WAS KNEELING on the hard earth floor of the house, frowning at the blackened circle of fire-stones. She had taken a big armful of the beech branches cut and stacked early that morning by Rima, and laid them criss-cross in the fireplace. A pile of sweet potatoes, large and small in their separate heaps, lay washed and ready to be roasted.

Jipona shook another match out of the box and struck it. It spurted briefly and fizzled out. She threw it crossly down to join a dozen others on the floor.

"Having trouble, girl?"

The old man Kian was peering in at the door, stooping down with his hands on his knees.

"The matches won't light, father," Jipona muttered. "Rima only brought this box up yesterday. I don't know what to do — Joseph will be back any time now, and you know how hungry he gets after school."

Rima ran a small trade-store, a tin hut which stood at the place where the track from the village joined the Highlands Highway. A truck from Mount Hagen, forty miles away, brought the goods for the store once a week. One of Rima's brothers drove it, unloading tins of fish, paraffin lamps, rolls of coloured cotton, bush knives and every kind of article the villagers might need. Rima didn't make much money out of the little store, but it gave him an important position among the village men. Now the rainy season was here, and the damp had crept into the store room, spoiling many of the goods.

Kian inspected the green box of matches.

"Poof! These are soaked. I've heard the same story all the way round the village. Your Rima isn't too popular, I can tell you."

"It isn't his fault, father," Jipona said indignantly.

Joseph burst into the house, his legs and feet spattered with mud from the road.

"Hallo, mother! Hallo, grandfather! I'm hungry!"

The old man laughed, and Jipona gave him a wry smile. Kian pinched his grandson's ear.

"You come with me and cut some sugar-cane to sharpen your teeth on. Then I'll show you how we used to make fire in the old days before the Europeans came."

While Joseph chewed on a length of green sugar-cane, sucking the sweet juices and spitting out the stringy fibres, Kian chose a dry branch from the fire-place with a slight kink in it. Unhurriedly the old man sat down and pared off the bark with his knife.

"Here — take my knife, and go and cut me a strip of bamboo — about as long as you — and mind it's dry!"

Joseph knew a place not far up the track where a clump of bamboos was sheltered by the tall forest trees. With his grandfather's knife he slit out a thin six-foot length of whippy, dry bamboo, and ran with it back to the hut.

Kian had prepared a pile of tindery bark. He set the peeled branch so that the little heap of shavings lay under the kinked part, and passed the strip of bamboo under the kink. Then he stood up, planted a foot firmly on each end of the branch to hold it down, and gripped the ends of the bamboo in each fist.

"This is hard work for an old man," he grinned at Jipona.

"I remember. You be careful, father."

Kian began to saw the bamboo strip up and down, his arms rising and falling in alternate strokes, his back bent. Soon a wisp of white smoke rose from the kink in the branch and a burning smell drifted to Joseph's nostrils. Grandfather went on sawing away, breathing heavily.

"Look! Look! Sparks!" Joseph cried. Red dots began to fall on to the pile of bark shavings. Kian grunted with satisfaction. Beads of sweat trickled down his forehead and into his beard. With a crackling noise, a tiny yellow flame licked round the heap of tinder. Another one flickered up.

Jipona grabbed Joseph's arm.

"Come on! Get down on your knees and blow!"

"Gently! Gently!" panted the old man as Joseph and his mother

blew the flames into life. Kian stopped sawing and straightened his back, puffing with his exertions. Jipona laid a small branch from the fire-place across the flames, and it caught alight. Joseph capered around the room as Jipona put the burning branch with the rest of the wood.

"Fire! *Fire!*"

After the sweet potatoes had been roasted and eaten, and the family were sitting round the fire, Rima began to complain about the ruin of his stores.

"I've lost three whole bags of rice, and all those skirts you made up, Jipona. Fifty kinas' worth of damage at least. How is a man supposed to make money if the bad spirits send so much rain?"

"I'll give you a hand tomorrow," offered Kian. "There are some sheets of tin near the new hotel at Banz — the builders left them behind. We'll need Kaipel's truck, though."

"Yes — he owes me a favour," Rima agreed. "We'll fix them on the back wall near the ground. That should keep out the wet."

He looked over at his son.

"Like to come?"

"He should be going to school," Jipona objected.

"He won't get far down the Highlands Highway in this," Rima said, looking out of the door at the pouring rain. The village square was a muddy pool in which pigs were splashing as they turned over the soil, looking for scraps.

"They should build a school here."

Joseph hugged his knees in delight. A day off school, and a trip with his father and grandfather to Banz in Kaipel's truck!

"We made fire today, didn't we, young fellow?" the old man said to Joseph. He smiled, looking down at the cigarette he was rolling.

"They teach you a lot in that school of yours, don't they? But have they ever told you how fire first came up to the Highlands? Eh?"

Joseph knew a story was coming. He shook his head and waited as Kian slowly settled himself into a comfortable position, and licked the cartoon section of the *Post-Courier* to close it round the cylinder of shredded tobacco. He picked up a glowing ember, and puffed the cigarette into flame. Then he nodded to his grandson.

"I wouldn't be able to enjoy this smoke if it hadn't been for a lazy pig and a clever dog . . . "

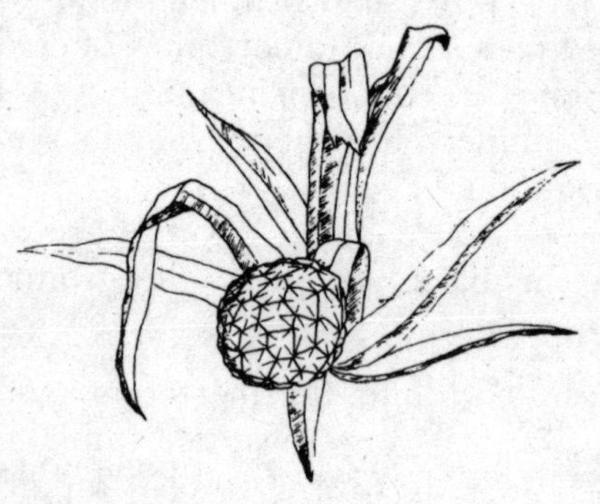

A very long time ago, before the two ancestors Kum Kopi and Nokpa formed the Kopi Nokpa clan, there was no fire in the Highlands. The people ate their sweet potatoes raw, and no-one could bear to try the flesh of pigs. When men came to a dark cave on a hunting expedition in the bush, none of them dared to go inside and explore for fear of the evil spirits that might be lurking there in the shadows. In the rainy season, the women shivered at home in their cold houses. Worst of all were the nights; no songs were sung or stories told. As soon as the evening meal was eaten, everybody lay down in the dark and shook with fear as the demons came whispering through the trees and danced all night outside.

In Womkama village in the mountains of the Chimbu lived Num and his wife Nala. Of all the dark and dreary places in those dark and dreary days, Womkama was the darkest and the dreariest. No light penetrated the dense leaves of the jungle that filled the valley in which the village lay. All day long the villagers wore the "Highlands overcoat" — hugging their necks with arms crossed tightly over their chests to keep out the damp and chill. Num and Nala had lived in Womkama village all their lives, and they had never heard of fire.

"I can't eat this," Num would say as he tried to swallow the hard white lumps of raw yam.

"What can I do about it?" shivered Nala, rubbing her cold legs.

Num and Nala owned two animals: Yakes, the cleverest dog in the whole of the Chimbu, and Obo, a lazy, fat, good-for-nothing pig. While Yakes scampered merrily around his master on their hunting trips, chased bush rats towards Num's sharp spear and helped Nala to dig up taro in the garden, Obo scratched his bristly back against a tree-stump, ate his own weight of vegetables every day and snapped at Num and Nala if they came too close.

One day a stranger came to Womkama village, trading beautiful pearly kina shells in exchange for the peanuts that were grown by the villagers. When he had a sackful, the stranger began to look around him at the cold, gloomy people.

"Why doesn't someone make a fire?" he asked

Num, who was passing with Yakes at his heels.

"Fire?" Num scratched his head in puzzlement. "What is that?"

The man stared at him.

"Fire, man! You know!"

"Never heard of it," Num mumbled.

The stranger couldn't believe his ears.

"You've never heard of fire? That's the most extraordinary thing I've ever heard. No wonder you all look half-starved and frozen!" And the stranger burst out laughing.

Num began to get angry.

"I don't know what you're laughing at. Don't think we like living like animals. What is this wonderful thing we've never heard of?"

"Fire?" said the man, sitting down on a log by the pig fence. "It's the most marvellous thing in the whole world. I live by the sea — I suppose you've never heard of that either — well, it's a place over there beyond the mountains, where the water starts and goes on for ever. We have fire there, plenty of it; too much, sometimes, when the wind decides to feed our houses to the flames. It's yellow and orange and red — it crackles and hisses among the branches. It makes my mouth water just to think of a big yam, cooked in the fire and pulled out roasting hot. You peel off the skin and eat the soft yellow flesh inside, tossing it from hand to hand to stop your fingers getting blistered. And a pig, now — put in a pit with stones from the beach and a smouldering red fire on top, covered with leaves and baked for a day — man, the smell! The warm juice runs down your chin, and you can't stop licking your fingers. *Ai! Ai!*"

Num groaned, thinking of the warm pig-juice and the smell that made the stranger cry, "*Ai! Ai!*"

"Then at night," the man went on, "all the village gathers round the fire, warm and friendly. Stories and songs pour out of people like sap from a tree. No-one is afraid of the dark in my tribe. The bad spirits stay on their mountain tops where I come from!"

He struck his brown chest with his fist and grinned at Num. "I tell you this, my friend — you get yourselves some fire. It's the best friend I know of, day or night."

He got up and shouldered his sack.

"Well, I've got what I came for. Goodbye! Wait till I tell my brother — I've actually met a man who's never heard of fire!"

Num watched the man striding out down the forest track. He looked tall and healthy as he swung along; a contrast to the sickly, constantly shivering inhabitants of Womkama.

By the time he had remembered to ask the stranger how to make this wonderful magic, he was long out of sight among the trees. Num ran after him, calling out, "Wait! Wait!", but there was no sign of the sturdy man and his sack.

Nala was furious when Num told her what he had learned.

"Why couldn't you have asked him to show you? Sometimes I think the cold is getting to your brains!" she shouted, and threw a handful of taros at him. Yakes the dog picked them up in his teeth and brought them back to her.

"At least there's someone in this house with a bit of sense," Nala snapped. She too had been entranced by thoughts of a hot fire, cheerful evenings and savoury pig-juice on her fingers. *Ai! Ai!*

Num looked at fat Obo, stretched out snoring in his hut.

“He can earn his living for a change,” he declared. He prodded Obo in the ribs and shouted into his ear, “Listen to me! Tomorrow morning you’ll go out and fetch us some fire. You heard what that stranger had to say — it’s over the mountains by the water which goes on for ever. I don’t care how you do it — but just you bring us back some fire, if you want to fill your belly again!”

Obo grunted crossly. The last thing he wanted was a long walk through the bush with no chance of a decent meal.

Next morning Obo pretended to have a stomach-ache. He moaned and rolled from side to side on his bed of leaves, looking up piteously at Num and Nala from his sly little eyes. But Nala twisted his tail round a stick, and Num grabbed him firmly by the nose. They were standing no nonsense from Obo when there was fire to be fetched.

Obo sulked as he dawdled along the forest paths. He felt tired and hungry. Why should he go all the way to the coast? He didn’t mind raw yams. The cold winds could not penetrate his thick hide; and as for evil spirits in the dark — *maski!* Obo didn’t believe in such rubbish.

He came to a river, wide and deep, that flowed across the track. Pigs won’t swim unless they have to, and Obo could please himself. He munched some bananas from a fallen tree, drank at the water’s edge and grubbed himself a bed in the earth. Why walk when you can sleep? Obo slept.

When he opened his eyes, it was night. Somewhere near, the undergrowth was rustling; a big animal must be stealthily pushing through the grass. A shining pair of eyes looked out at Obo. A loud screech echoed among the silent trees. Obo jumped up. Evil spirits?

— nonsense! Still, it was wise to take precautions. He began to walk back the way he had come, staring nervously round him at the inscrutable jungle. More eyes gleamed between the tree trunks, and the rustling noise became louder. Obo began to trot, his heavy body banging into low branches. A blood-curdling shriek rang out behind him. They were coming to get him!

Stout Obo galloped through the forest. He blundered along the path, snorting in terror. He hadn't run so fast since he was a piglet. Eyes, rustles and catcalls haunted him until the dawn light began to filter through the trees. Then the night beasts of the jungle called off the game, and went back sniggering to their dens and caves.

Womkama village lay just ahead. Obo collapsed among the bushes, his flanks heaving as his breath came slowly back. He hadn't been frightened, of course — just taking his part sportingly in the game. Demons in the bush? — poof! There was no sense in staying here, all the same; he might as well get back to the village. Now — what was this fire business all about? He hadn't bothered to listen when Num was explaining. Something red — that was all he could remember. He'd have to take something back to Num and Nala unless he wanted a beating. Some red flowers growing a short distance away from the path caught Obo's eye. He pulled away a string of them and slouched on, out of the bush and into the village.

Num was waiting at the door of his hut. When he caught sight of fat Obo, the scarlet flowers twined round his shoulders and floating out behind, he shouted with laughter. Nala came out to see what all the noise was about; but she didn't laugh. She snatched up a stick, and gave Obo a tremendous hiding.

"You didn't even try, did you? I might have known it! Now get in your pen and keep out of my way!"

Then she turned on Num.

"And you should have realised that lazy ne'ér-do-well would get it wrong. For the sake of the spirits of our ancestors, send Yakes this time! That dog's the only one with any common sense."

Yakes the dog didn't wait to be told twice. He shot off like an arrow down the path. He swam the rivers, climbed the mountains and jumped over the waterfalls. He dodged wild boars, fought crocodiles and bit snakes in two. He didn't stop for food or rest until he had run a hundred miles through the jungle, right down from the Highlands to the coast. Even there he didn't stand staring at the wide blue sea — not Yakes! He trotted along the beach and snapped up a crab for his breakfast. When he came to a village, he lay down in the sand and slept two suns and moons away.

Yakes woke to a pink sunset sky and the sound of singing. The village men had lit a huge fire on the beach and the whole clan was gathered around it. Yakes lay in the sand and looked at the leaping flames and listened to the deep-throated songs. For several hours he waited, watching the feast and licking his chops as the new and delicious fragrance of roast meat reached his nostrils. At last the chattering, laughing groups of people broke up and families wandered off to their houses, leaving the fire unguarded on the shore.

Then Yakes crept warily up. He looked around, but all was still. Yakes found a bone in the sand, still warm from the roasting, and crunched in ecstacy. Then he sniffed at the fire, and gingerly picked up the end of a burning branch in his mouth, wrinkling up his nose to stop his whiskers from singeing. Quietly the little dog trotted up the beach with the flaming stick and vanished among the palm trees. No-one saw him go.

Nala put down her digging stick, and collected all the yams she had dug up from the garden that day. She piled them into her string bag and bent down to slip the headband round her forehead. As she straightened up with the heavy load on her back, a strange sight caught her attention. Far away in the forest a thin column of smoke was drifting up from the tree-tops. As Nala watched, she saw the smoke moving slowly towards her. She took off the bag of yams and stared hard.

"Num! Num! Come and look at this," she cried out. Num heard her from where he was grinding a sharp edge on to a stone axe-head, and came up at a run. He gazed at the column of smoke, then clapped his hands and laughed out loud.

"It must be Yakes! Good dog! He's brought us fire!"

Yakes appeared on the bush track; he seemed to be holding the end of the smoky cloud in his teeth, where a glowing red light was burning. He ran up to Num and Nala, and dropped the fire-stick in front of them. Yakes sneezed — the ashes had got up his nose, and his fine whiskers were shrivelled and black.

Num bent down and picked up the stick by the red end. Next instant he dropped it, and howled loudly enough to bring all the villagers running from houses and gardens. Num danced, and sucked his burnt fingers.

"Fool!" exclaimed Nala.

She picked up the branch by the other end and ran with it down the track to the house.

"What is it? A bad spirit? Something has bitten Num!" shouted the excited villagers as they followed.

Nala rounded on them.

"Quickly — if you want to be warm and well fed tonight! This fire is nearly dead. Get plenty of dry sticks — hurry!"

A pile was soon collected by eager hands, and the precious fire-stick carefully pushed into the middle. Everyone yelled and leapt with delight as the flames crackled up. More and more branches were brought. A group of young men raced off into the bush and dragged a rotten tree-trunk back to the village clearing. By nightfall the biggest fire ever seen in the Chimbu from that day to this was blazing red and yellow, and all Womkama village toasted its hands and roasted its yams round the flames. Children jumped for joy, and burned their mouths on hot food for the first but not the last time. The best singer in the village made up a fifty verse song in honour of Yakes the dog, and sang it all night. Only the disgruntled Obo sulked and snorted among his damp leaves. Fire? *Maski!*

When the fire and feasting began to die down, the villagers took flaming sticks back to their own houses and started their own fires. Seven huts went up in flames before the people learned to treat the new toy with respect. Nala made a circle of stones in the centre of the floor to hold the fire, and Num hacked out a hole in the roof when the smoke stung their eyes. He and Nala gorged themselves on sweet hot yams until they could eat no more. Yakes had a place of honour near the fire — wasn't it he who had brought the magic thing from the place beyond the mountains where the water starts and goes on for ever? Num even took out a pile of cooked yams for Obo in his shed, but Obo turned his back and showed his teeth over his shoulder. He couldn't see what all the fuss was about.

Soon fire had spread all over the Chimbu, and people carried it from there to every corner of the Highlands. The men learned how to saw sparks from a dry branch with a strip of bamboo. The women found many ways of cooking with hot ashes and stones. The hunters explored the darkest caves with flaring torches. The bad spirits stayed on their mountain-tops; and the nights, free of fear, were filled with songs and stories.

Yet the people remembered Num and Nala of Womkama village, and Yakes the clever dog. His descendants — and they are as many as the leaves in the forest — take as their right the warmest place nearest to the fire in every house in Papua New Guinea.

But the descendants of Obo the pig — and they are as many as the seeds of the passion-fruit — have a different place of honour among the people. *Ai! Ai!*

HOW LAI AND AMBUM JOINED THE SEPIK

THE WAHGI WAS IN full spate. Kian Kombuk and Joseph sat side by side, watching the rain-swollen river surging past their toes. Thirty yards across, the coffee-coloured flood swept round a bend, sucking at the earth and stones of the banks. A whole tree went rolling by, the bare roots sticking up above the leaf-strewn surface, leaving a trail of bubbles in its wake. Five days and nights of continuous rain over the mountains had raised the level of the river to within a couple of feet of the grassland, and a brown muddy stain was already creeping outwards across the plain.

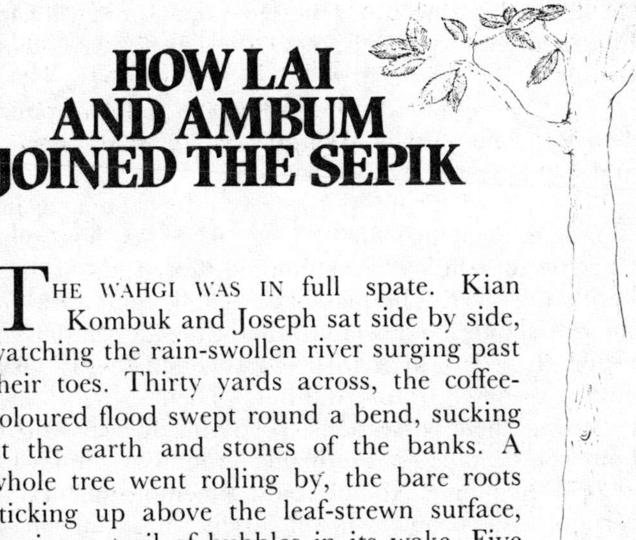

It was an afternoon in the school holidays, and the old man had brought his grandson down to the river to watch the flood. Joseph had brought his new fishing line and hooks, but the powerful current was pulling the light nylon line almost horizontal, and the fish had hidden themselves deep under the banks to ride out the spate.

At last Joseph hauled in his line and rolled it round a stick, pushing the hooks into a leaf for safe keeping, and sat back to enjoy the spectacle.

"Quite a sight, isn't it?" observed the old man as he stared at the racing water. "There'll be a few houses in there by tonight," and he pointed to a group of huts beside the river. The pigs had already come in from the grasslands, and were gathered inside the fence, lifting their feet high to avoid the puddles as they circled restlessly round the huts. Their owners were collecting their possessions, preparing to leave their homes and make for the higher ground at the lower edge of the jungle. No-one could remember such rain; certainly the people who had built those huts had never expected Old Man Wahgi to leave his bed and chase them away.

Kian got to his feet and ruefully inspected the wet mud clinging to his legs.

"Ugh! We'll be in there too, if we don't look out. Wahgi must have been taking a few lessons from Lai!"

"Lai?" Joseph looked up at his grandfather as they started back on the walk to Kopi village.

"Lai. The one who had the race with Ambum. He had good sport with the people that night!" He jerked his thumb over his shoulder in the direction of the threatened houses. Joseph looked back and saw a crowd of men shepherding the pigs out of the compound and along a track that led to the hills.

Their anxious shouts came faintly over the roar of the flooding river. Behind them pattered a group of women and children, even the smallest of whom were helping to carry bundles and sacks away from the danger area.

"They haven't learned the lesson of that tale, have they?" murmured the old man.

Joseph had heard the story before; it was one of the first that Kian had told him. Now the sight of the swollen Wahgi and its cargo of flotsam had awakened the old man's tongue. The rain had stopped, and a watery sun was shining above the black clouds that had filled the skies all week. When they reached the Highlands Highway, the puddles in the pot-holes were gleaming like mirrors. The story lasted all the way back to the village, and Joseph forgot his disappointment at having no fish to show Jipona as he listened to his grandfather unfolding the tale of Lai and Ambum, and their journey to the mighty Sepik River.

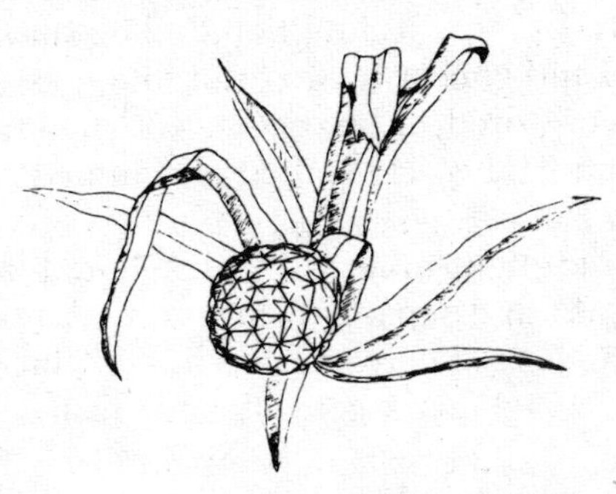

High up in the mountains of the Highlands two pools lived side by side in a clearing in the bush. Their names were Lai and Ambum and their natures were as different as the seasons. Lai was a rough, boisterous fellow. He liked to jump and splash whenever a breeze blew. He was wide and shallow, and left his bed at the least excuse to invade the holes of the bush rats and chase the tree pythons up into the branches.

The animals of the forest avoided Lai, for whenever they lowered their mouths to his surface he would surge up and make them splutter and sneeze. They preferred to gather in the evening at Ambum's calm brink and take their drink in peace; for Ambum lay deep and still.

At night the yellow moon slid across the clearing and looked down at two reflections, one splintered and broken, the other flat and motionless. Lai knew all the chatter and rumour of the forest, and gossiped in whispers and giggles, while silent Ambum kept his own counsel. It was strange to see such unlikely companions pass their time together. Yet the mountain spirit had set them in their place, and there they stayed, a few yards apart, until the day of the expedition.

One day Lai was feeling bored. The bush rats had packed up and gone away to drier lodgings. The other animals were tired of his tricks, and had not visited him for many days. He shifted and fumed among the reeds.

"Hey, old tight-mouth!" Lai shouted across the strip of grass that separated him from Ambum. "I'm fed up lying here. There's no fun in this place since the rats went away. Let's get out and push a few trees over!"

Ambum smiled and stayed quiet.

"Come on, you dull puddle! Don't just sit there dreaming. Let's have a game!" fussed Lai, uprooting a bunch of reeds and kicking them out onto the bank.

"Why not lie still and listen to the birds in the trees?" suggested Ambum.

"Birds in the trees? What a bore!" Lai swirled round and round his hollow. Then he stopped so suddenly that he sucked himself into a whirlpool, and had to wait until he was calm enough to get his idea out.

"I know! Let's have a race! We could run right down to the Sepik River and hitch a ride to the sea. What do you say?"

Now Ambum had heard plenty of stories from the birds about the mighty Sepik River that wound its way hundreds of miles northwards from the mountains to the coast. He had heard of the great swamps with their forests of tiny trees, and the narrow gorges high up in the hills where the water boiled white and hissed over rocks; of the men of the Sepik and their tall decorated houses for their gods, their wooden war shields painted with staring faces, and the long outrigger canoes of the coastal tribes. Suddenly a burning desire awoke in the depths of Ambum at Lai's challenge: to ride to the sea with the master river, to race over rocks and meander through marshy plains, to see the boats and the fierce men of Sepik. He looked around at the glade he knew so well, its tall trees backed by the blue mountain peaks. If he agreed to go with Lai, part of him would always stay here to feed the river he would become. He would not be leaving his home for ever.

"I'll come," said Ambum, "but I don't want to race you. We must be careful not to spoil the gardens the people have made down below in the valley, or wreck the animals' homes. We can find a safe path through the bush, well away from anyone, and flow quietly down together."

"Oh, very well," Lai muttered. He wanted a companion for the journey, to brag to and impress with a show of strength and speed; and Ambum was the only possible choice. "Let's go, then."

Lai began to stream out of his bed and down the mountainside.

"Wait!" called Ambum. "Don't be so hasty. We haven't thought out the way we're going yet. Let's each plan out a route tonight, and we can make a final decision tomorrow morning. You don't want to set off without giving it some thought."

"All right, all right," grumbled Lai, squeezing his turbulent body back into the confines of his hollow. "Really, you do make a fuss about a simple idea."

That night, while Ambum lay thinking out the least destructive route for the journey, Lai grew more and more impatient. What were a few miserable rat-holes and gardens anyway? He, Lai, was about to become a river! You can't make a river without flooding a few rat-holes.

At last he could stand it no longer. He looked over at Ambum, but the quiet pool was deep in thought, planning for tomorrow. Stealthily, Lai crept out of his bed and trickled down the slope. The moon glinted on his newly sinuous shape, but Ambum noticed nothing. When his head was well out of sight of the glade, Lai stopped and grinned to himself. Ambum would get a shock at sun-rise! Let the old slowcoach keep to the deep jungle if he liked — Lai wasn't so finicky!

Lai puffed out his head and gathered all his length into a tall, powerful wave. He paused a moment, savouring his new-found strength — then plunged downwards, foaming and roaring through the bush. He burst on the first village like a dragon, tearing down the flimsy wooden fence and rampaging through the huts, sweeping them to right and left. Women, men and children screamed and ran for their lives as

Lai raced on, bowling over dogs and pigs, uprooting trees and sending boulders spinning into the forest. He pushed his wet fingers into the bush rats' holes, drowning whole families where they lay, and knocked the tree kangaroos off the branches. Cassowaries, taken by surprise, woke to find themselves swimming up to their necks in Lai's flood.

A second and a third village were battered to pieces as Lai thundered down the valley. There was no time to raise the alarm; no time for anything but panic and flight. Lai laughed aloud to see the people climbing trees in terror, or running madly away as he hissed at their heels. In the dark he was more fearsome than an earthquake. This was life — this was what he was made for! Kau-kaus, bananas, peanuts, corn — all were jumbled together in his grasp and flung far into the jungle as the gardens that had been so painstakingly made were obliterated in seconds. A cloud of birds rose squawking from the tree tops and flew above his head, marking his trail of destruction.

As dawn came up, Lai saw below him the Sepik River itself, curving majestically at the foot of the mountains. Lai dashed in among the trees that fringed the water and drew up, panting from the long night's run. Wheeee! What a chase! What marvellous fun! Now he would rest up and wait for Ambum, and have a good laugh when the old lie-abed finally arrived. He would take his time over the plunge into the Sepik; it would look better if the master river could compare them both as they flowed in side by side — dull old Ambum, and sparkling, vigorous Lai!

Miles away in the mountains, Ambum had planned out the last details of the path they would follow. They could wind in and out of the trees, skirting villages and keeping to the dry gullies of old streams where there was no earth for animals' burrows. It might take all day, but they would be sure of causing no disturbance.

For some time there had been an unaccustomed silence from the hollow where Lai was usually to be heard babbling and splashing. Ambum called out, "I think I've worked out the best route. How about you?"

There was no reply.

"Have you had any good ideas? Let's run through them before we set out."

No sound came from Lai's bed, but a Bird of Paradise who was perched in a tree let out a raucous burst of laughter.

"Take a look, Ambum!" he cackled. "Take a look!"

Ambum heaved himself up to grass level and looked over at the opposite hollow. It was empty. A silvery spring bubbled from the mud in the middle.

Ambum slid forward and peered over the rim of his bed. A wide channel had been carved in the mountainside, in which a shallow stream sparkled. A mile below, trees lay uprooted on each side, and the remains of a pig-fence and several huts were entangled in the lower branches of the forest.

"He's gone! He's gone! What a joke! What a joke!" screeched the Bird of Paradise from his perch.

Ambum flowed over the lip of the hollow, and began to roll down the slope. As he followed the path of Lai's mad race, Ambum could see the destruction that had been wrought. People were standing around in grim silence, shaking their heads over the ruin of their village. Children gathered soaking possessions from the mud — a stick doll, smeared with mud; a sodden sleeping-mat. The bodies of drowned pigs, dogs and wild animals were everywhere. Some of the men shook their fists at Ambum as he went past, but when they saw that he meant them no harm they turned resignedly back to the weary business of salvage.

Below the first village, Ambum stopped and considered. It was clear that Lai had tricked him and run riot during the night. There was only one place where Lai could have made for if he meant to join the Sepik — the swamplands at the foot of the mountain range. Very well: Ambum would follow the route he had planned, which would bring him out at the same spot. Then, when he caught up with Lai, he would let him know just what he thought of his behaviour.

Sad and silent, Ambum wound through the bush, taking care to keep his distance from the villages along the way. In some places he had to double back on himself to avoid a garden or isolated house, but he stuck to his plan and troubled no living thing on his twisting journey northwards. He travelled three times as far as Lai, and it was late in the evening when at last he emerged from the trees and saw the setting sun glittering on the broad back of Sepik. By its side, half hidden among the bushes, Ambum made out the self-important figure of Lai, now transformed into a silver snake that coiled down from the jungle, its head ready to strike into the flank of the great river.

"Hallo, slowcoach! Where have you been?" shouted Lai cheerfully as Ambum flowed through the swampy grass to join him.

"I've been taking more care than you," retorted Ambum. "What do you mean by sneaking off in the middle of the night and smashing up everything in sight?"

Lai was too full of himself to listen.

"I had a marvellous run — straight as an arrow,

and never stopped till I got here. I've been waiting all day for you, you sluggard!"

Ambum glared at him. "And do you know how many villages you wrecked on your marvellous run?"

"Oh, pooh — villages!" snorted Lai. "Who cares about stupid men and their rotten old huts? I beat you in our race, anyway. You're jealous, that's your trouble."

Quiet Ambum was usually the calmest of fellows, but now he lost his temper.

"Jealous, am I, you thoughtless oaf?" he shouted. "You don't think of anyone but yourself!"

Lai swelled up with indignation. His head furrowed the grass as he hissed menacingly forward. He thrust out a long arm and gave Ambum a hard shove. The two rivers mingled and parted as they pushed and jostled on the brink of the Sepik. Suddenly Ambum grabbed Lai by the head, and they fell locked together down the bank and into the master river. In a moment the angry pair were swallowed up in the main stream, and were carried onwards through the swamplands to the sea.

You can still see the straight, roaring path of Lai down the mountainside, and the winding, curving track of Ambum as he makes his careful way down to the Sepik. They still struggle together at the edge of the river before tumbling in each other's grasp into that all-embracing tide; and then the quarrel is forgotten as they are hurried down to the sea.

But the people who live in that region will never forget the story of Lai and Ambum: for while Ambum never causes any trouble, Lai still leaves his narrow bed now and then for another romp through the bush; and men say as they clear up after him, "Some things never change — and Lai is one of them, curse him!"

WHY CASSOWARIES DON'T FLY

RIMA STEPPED BACK and looked critically at his handiwork. He grunted with satisfaction, and smiled down at his son.

"Well?"

The new hut stood foursquare in the corner of the garden. The plaited bamboo walls curled tightly round a stout frame of beech poles, cut and stripped by Rima with the big bush knife he had brought up from the trade-store when Joseph had run down to tell him the news.

"It's marvellous, father," said Joseph. "She won't get out of that."

He bent down and stroked the shining plumage of a large bird that lay at his feet, trussed up with creepers. The bonds were too tight to allow the muscular body any movement, but the bird crossly jerked its head and opened its pointed beak to hiss at Joseph's fingers. The face and neck were coloured bright blue and red, and the head was topped with an oval dome of bone. The feathers were long and limp, hanging in silky strands. Under the creeper bindings twitched stumps of flightless wings.

"That's a fine cassowary," Rima remarked. "Did

she give you much trouble?"

"No: after all, there were eight of us. *Aieee!* She ran like the wind!"

The village boys had caught the cassowary that morning, coming on her suddenly in the bush and chasing her down a long slope. Her strong legs were capable of taking her clear of pursuers on the level or going uphill. But once she was on a downward incline she could only run faster and faster, squawking with fury as she lost her balance, till she tripped over and fell in a tumble of feathers and feet.

Then Joseph and another boy, outrunning the others, had flung themselves on top of the flapping bird and held her down, while the remaining young hunters had torn down bush creepers for rope. The trickiest part was keeping the feet with their fearsome claws underneath the body while she was lashed up

like a parcel. The whooping and laughing boys carried her back to the village, her head dangling down from a branch slotted between her feet. Joseph and the other boy had drawn playing cards for her, and Joseph's ten of hearts had just beaten David Mali's nine of diamonds.

Joseph was overjoyed to have his own cassowary. She would always be bad-tempered, liable to peck out an eye or lash out dangerously with those sharp claws. But safely shut in her new home, fed on taro scraps and berries, she would grow fat; and one day in the future she would make a tough but tasty roast for a clan gathering. Then the story of the capture would be told, with Joseph as the hero.

"Ready? Let's get her inside. I'll hold her, and you cut the ropes — here, take my knife. Watch out, now —she's in a bad mood."

Rima picked up the cassowary in his strong arms and clasped the hard thigh muscles with both hands while Joseph sawed through the creepers. The big bird squatted quietly against Rima's chest, but her eyes held a sulky, defiant glare. Rima waddled with his burden towards the little hut, which he had purposely built without a door; the cassowary would not be coming out again before her day of doom. A small window about four feet from the ground provided the only entrance, and Rima rested the bird's weight against the frame while Joseph stood on tiptoe beside him to watch.

With a heave of both arms and chest Rima pushed the cassowary through the window. As she fell into the dark interior of the hut, one cramped leg came free for a moment, and in that split second the bird kicked out viciously. The long middle claw on her foot tore a gash in Rima's arm and spots of blood began to well up on the brown skin.

"Ai!"

Rima cursed, and brushed away the blood with his other hand. He grabbed Joseph roughly by the shoulder as the boy peered in at the window, and pulled him away.

"Get back! Do you want to lose an eye?"

From the inside of the hut came a thumping and screeching as the cassowary tested her dungeon. The whole building shook, and some grass fell from the roof; but Rima had built many cassowary huts, and this one stood up sturdily to the battering.

The window was too high up to be reached by the captive, though she could poke her head out to be fed. If these huts were strongly constructed, they made a foolproof prison for a flightless bird.

Rima rubbed his wounded arm.

"Give her some food and water tonight, when she's tired herself out," he advised. "But be careful, Joseph! Never trust one of those brutes."

He inspected the scratch. It was sore, but would heal up cleanly in a few days.

"Lucky it wasn't a male in the breeding season!"

"Why?" Joseph asked his favourite question.

"All that hot blood goes to their feet, that's why. Their main claws are full of poison. Makes a man's arm swell up like a rotten log. In the old days you were done for. Even now there are a few people waking up in Goroka hospital with only one arm, wishing they hadn't got between Mr. Cassowary and his girl-friends."

Joseph glanced up at his father as they walked down the path to the village. As usual, he wasn't sure whether Rima was joking. But his father's face was quite serious.

"You ask your grandfather about it tonight. He can tell you a tale or two about our friend in the hut."

Rima looked at the sun as it hung above the mountain tops.

"Come on, boy. I must get this scratch washed and tied up. Jipona will be waiting for you, too. Run!"

Kian Kombruk drew on his cigarette until the end glowed red.

"How did she like her supper?" he asked his grandson. Joseph hugged his knees by the fire.

"She ate it all, grandfather — at least I think she did. I didn't dare look in to see!"

Everyone laughed. Joseph ducked his head behind his arm, embarrassed. But Kian went on kindly, "I hear you were a little bolder in the bush this morning. It was a brave thing to do, jumping on a cassowary in full flight."

"A foolish thing to do," murmured Jipona. "He might have really hurt himself."

"I remember the first time I tried that," said Kian. "The old bird we were chasing just put on an extra spurt, and I banged my chin on the ground so hard I thought a tree had fallen on me!" The old man scratched his beard thoughtfully. "It's lucky they can't fly; otherwise we'd never get near them. And a cassowary's wing-bone through the nose of a handsome young fellow was a fine attraction for the girls once upon a time!"

Kian fingered the hole that his own father had pierced through the fleshy part of his nose between the nostrils when Kian had reached manhood. Joseph had seen his grandfather dressed up for a sing-sing with a long white bone through this hole, forming a kind of false moustache each side of his nose.

"But there was a time long ago when the cassowary could fly as well as the bower-bird," the old man rumbled as he reached for a sweetcorn in the cinders.

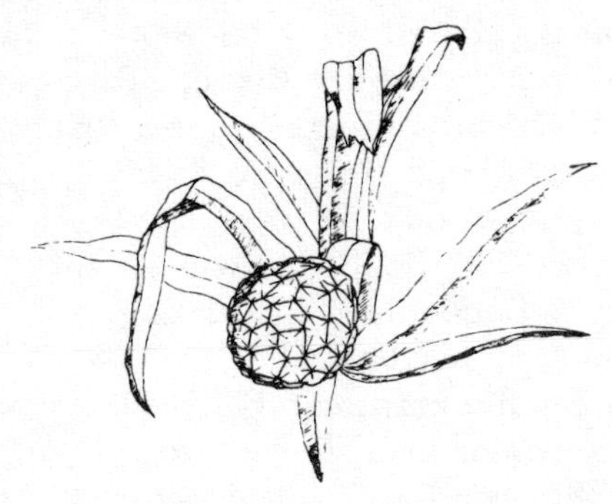

Cassowary and Bower-bird used to fly around together. Any morning you could see them tearing through the tree-tops, chasing each other up and down as they searched for the red berries that they loved. These berries, plump and sweet, grew on the bushes near the very top of the mountain. All the birds in the forest knew about them; but they took good care to keep away when Cassowary and Bower-bird came racketing through the jungle.

Bower-bird was normally a shy fellow, who lived deep in the bush in a little house he had made from leaves and moss, and decorated with brightly coloured pebbles and flowers. He kept himself to himself, and never bothered anyone. Then he struck up an acquaintance with Cassowary, and began to puff out his chest and give a beakful of cheek to everyone he met; even to wise old Owl himself! Cassowary taught him bad habits, but Cassowary didn't care — not he! All he wanted was a bellyful of berries and a chance to bully the small birds. When he flapped his stumpy wings and heaved his fat body up above the topmost branches, Cassowary was as pleased as pie. He sang as he flew — a croaking song, horrible to hear — but Cassowary didn't care. Not he! He smashed up the nests of the Birds of Paradise, and flew off laughing.

"That Cassowary will come to a bad end," grunted old Owl when he heard of the goings-on. "He's a sight too full of himself. He'll trip over his own wings one fine day, mark my words."

One day Cassowary flopped down into the clearing in front of Bower-bird's pretty little house.

"What's new?" he screeched.

"There's a batch of bushes in berry on the morning side of the mountain," said Bower-bird. "I saw them when I flew over yesterday."

Cassowary's little eyes sparkled with greed. The two companions flew off and were soon high above the jungle, cruising towards the mountain.

"Doesn't he look a fool?" sniggered the ground pigeons as the pair went overhead. Cassowary did look decidedly odd with his short wings flailing like paddles to keep his heavy body aloft, and his long legs treading the air beneath him. All the same, the ground pigeons were careful to keep well under cover. They had tasted Cassowary's sharp dagger of a beak before.

Soon the two partners had landed on the mountain top, and they got busy among the berry bushes. Bower-bird ate daintily, plucking one scarlet berry at a time from its bed of leaves, chewing it thoroughly in his short beak and swallowing before taking another. Cassowary behaved like the ruffian he was, tearing away whole clusters of berries and gorging them all at once, champing and crashing among the bushes. He spoiled twice as much fruit as he ate by crushing the berries beneath his clumsy feet in a mad rush from bush to bush. Bower-bird began to get impatient.

"Do be careful, Cassowary," he twittered peevishly. "You're wasting half of them!"

The only reply was a muffled crunching as Cassowary disposed of a beakful of berries, leaves and twigs. He ripped the last few berries off their bush, swallowed them in one gulp, and surveyed the mess he had made with satisfaction.

"That was good! What's next?" he demanded.

Bower-bird was furious. The berries had been his discovery, after all, and he had eaten hardly a dozen.

"It's time you learned a lesson, my friend," he muttered under his breath. Looking around, his glance fell on the twigs scattered on the ground where Cassowary had thrown them. Now Bower-bird, for all his small size, was a quick-witted fellow, and at once he thought of a trick to play on Cassowary.

"I'll show you what's next," he thought, and turned to Cassowary with his sweetest smile. "Er — why not sing me one of your lovely songs?"

Like many bullies, Cassowary was extremely vain. He loved the sound of his own singing, though no-one else did. He preened himself and smirked.

"Let's fly up into that tree over there," suggested Bower-bird. "Then the whole forest could enjoy your wonderful voice."

Cassowary lumbered up on to a branch and began to squawk, screwing his eyes tight shut, the better to appreciate his own performance. Bower-bird picked up two green twigs and hid them under his wings. Then he flew up beside Cassowary and pretended to be listening to the song. At last the big bully grated to a standstill, and opened his eyes to see the effect on his little friend.

"Wonderful! Quite marvellous!" enthused Bower-bird. "They must have heard you over in Wabag.

Truly the Cassowaries have the loudest — er, I mean the loveliest voices in all the world!"

"Yes, my family are very gifted," sighed Cassowary. "We are strong, brave, clever — and the gods have blessed us with magical voices, too."

He looked down at the little bird beside him. "It's a pity they seem to have forgotten you, my dear fellow. All you can do is poke bits of coloured stone about, eh?"

Bower-bird saw that his chance had come.

"Well, actually — that's not quite all we can do." He lowered his voice and glanced over his shoulder. "In fact, I'll let you into a secret, if you like. We're not supposed to tell anyone about it, but I don't mind you knowing."

"Oh, I won't tell a soul," promised the delighted Cassowary.

"Bend your head down here," murmured Bower-bird. Cassowary put his domed head close to Bower-bird's beak.

"We can break our bones and heal ourselves straight away," whispered the little bird. "All the Bower-birds can do it."

Cassowary straightened up and stared disbelievingly at him. "Break your bones and heal yourself? Nonsense! No-one can do that. I've never heard such rubbish!"

"It's true," Bower-bird said, nodding his head.

"Prove it, then," jeered Cassowary. "You're just making it up!"

Bower-bird smiled to himself. "Very well," he answered. "Suppose I were to break the bones in my wings, and then fly to the top of the mountain and back. Would you believe me then?"

"If you can do that," conceded Cassowary, "I'll

believe you — but you can't!"

Bower-bird sidled along the branch away from Cassowary. He didn't want the big fool overlooking his preparations. Pretending to mutter magic words to distract Cassowary's attention, he adjusted the green twigs under his wings. Then he began to press the twigs against the branch, groaning loudly and jabbering incantations. The twigs bent under the pressure, then splintered with a tearing crack.

Cassowary blinked in astonishment. It certainly seemed as if his friend had snapped the bones of both his wings. Then he gaped as Bower-bird fluttered the wings that should have been useless, and sprang into the air in a perfect take-off. Straight and fast flew Bower-bird as he made for the mountain top. Cassowary was too far away to see the two splintered twigs that fell from beneath the trickster's wings and vanished among the tree-tops. Bower-bird rolled and swooped to show off his flying skills before returning to land beside Cassowary on the branch. For once in his life, Cassowary was speechless.

Bower-bird smiled mockingly at him. "Now it's your turn," he said. "Come on — all you have to do is break your wings and fly! I'll say the magic words for you. Or are you scared?"

This suggestion went straight to the foolish Cassowary's head, as the cunning Bower-bird had planned. He looked down at his own stubby wings, while Bower-bird began to chant gibberish. Break his wing-bones? Well — if a little squirt of a Bower-bird could do it — so could a Cassowary!

He pressed the tips of his wings against the branch and leaned his full weight on them.

"Ow! Ow! It hurts!"

"That's only because you've had no practice,"

Bower-bird said reassuringly. He choked back his laughter as he watched the wincing Cassowary bending his wings.

"I thought you were good at everything. The ground pigeons will laugh themselves sick when I tell them you couldn't even break your own bones — you've broken enough of theirs!"

This prospect made Cassowary mad with rage. He jerked downwards with the powerful muscles of his shoulders. Snap! went the bones of his wings.

"Ai! Aieeee!" squealed Cassowary.

"Now, my good friend — fly!" shouted Bower-bird, and gave the heavy body a hard push. Cassowary rocked and swayed, digging his toes desperately into the branch. Then he lost his balance and fell backwards, tumbling like a sack of yams to the ground below.

Bower-bird opened his beak, threw back his head and laughed until the tears came.

"Ohé, Cassowary — why don't you fly?" he called down. Cassowary heaved about in the grass. He got to his feet and tried to fly up to get at Bower-bird, but every time he leaped into the air he fell back to earth.

"You devil! You've tricked me! I can't fly!" wailed Cassowary. "Just wait till I get up there!"

He took a run at the tree trunk, and scrambled a few feet up before pitching on his head. Bower-bird laughed and laughed.

"Eh, great flyer! Why don't you fly? Eaten too many berries?"

Just then a man, attracted by all the noise and commotion, came out of the jungle and began to climb up the mountain side towards Cassowary.

"Here's a friend for you, Cassowary," chortled Bower-bird. "Ask him if he knows the magic words! Farewell, great flyer!"

Then Bower-bird spread his wings and flew away to tell the world the news of the downfall of Cassowary. Old Owl mumbled, "I knew it! He tripped over his own wings, just as I said."

And the wise old bird, who had seen many a bully brought low in the twenty years since he was hatched, clicked his beak and closed his eyes.

SAMBOLI PLAYS A TRICK

UNDER THE TREES AT THE corner of the village square, the Saturday Council meeting was breaking up. Groups of elderly men were standing around, chatting, laughing and discussing the various plans that had been made. In spite of the hot sunshine, most of them wore their peaked caps with the red bands that marked them out as village Councillors. Not one of the men was under fifty years of age; Rima would have to wait at least another ten years before he would be eligible to take his place among the experienced men of the Council.

Berom Kibunke, the leader of the Council and a "big-man" in the Kopi Nokpa clan, called a cheerful farewell as he climbed into the battered Toyota truck driven by one of his sons and bounced away in a cloud of dust down the track towards the Highlands Highway. Joseph, watching from his seat on a tree trunk outside the pig-fence, saw his grandfather take off his cap and scratch his grey woolly hair as he exchanged a parting word with Ua, his oldest friend and fellow Councillor. Now the meeting was over, Joseph could find out the answer to the question that loomed largest in his mind at the moment. He raced down the hillside towards the square. Kian Kombuk saw him coming, and threw up his arm in mock terror.

"It's the elephant, Ua! Run for your life!"

The whole village was still talking about the star attraction at that year's Highlands Show. Twenty thousand people had come from all over Papua New Guinea to Mount Hagen for a long week-end of singing and dancing. Each tribe was dressed in its traditional costume — Asaro mud-men with their white clay helmets and bodies, Sepik River tribes decorated with thousands of tiny sea-shells, warriors from Wabag in human hair wigs. On the last afternoon, after the judging of the finals of the dancing contest, a large cargo plane had landed in the great arena. The folding doors in the nose of the plane were opened, and out trundled an enormous grey monster with a nose that touched the ground and ears like giant taro leaves. Joseph, perched on Rima's shoulders in the crowd, had recognised the elephant from pictures in his school book, and let out a scream of excitement that turned the heads of those nearby. Then he joined in the laugh that rose from twenty thousand throats as the elephant solemnly went down on one knee and saluted the crowd with upraised trunk.

"Grandfather! What did Berom Kibunke say?"

Kian caught hold of Joseph by the shoulders and swung him round to face Ua.

"Here, Ua! Here's the source of all the trouble."

Ua was a cheerful man with a big stomach and a deep, rumbling voice. He liked to growl and play the ogre with the village children. He stroked his beard and frowned menacingly down at Joseph.

"It's you, is it, you little villain? And just why do you think we should spend all this money on this new

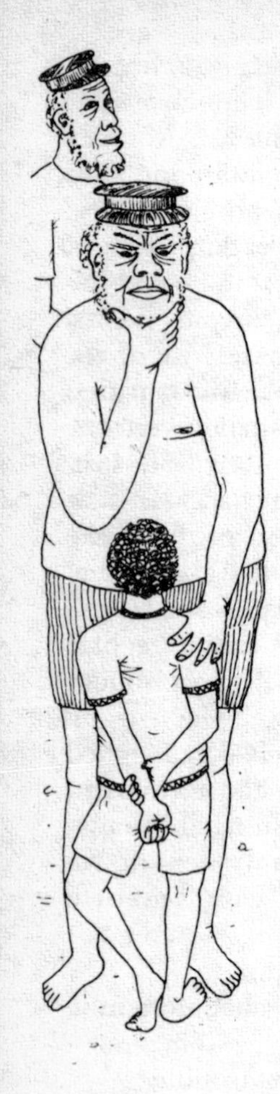

classroom of yours? Eh?"

He winked at Kian and squatted down on his haunches to bring his face on a level with Joseph's, his belly folding into plump creases. "Well, boy, you seem to have turned your grandfather's head — and he has turned Berom Kibunke's."

"Then the Council will give Brother Tim the money ?" Joseph asked Kian breathlessly.

"Yes, my little elephant — you can take seventy kinas to him on Monday."

"Seventy kinas! *Ai!*" Joseph had never held twenty kinas in his hand before. He turned a cartwheel, and dashed away to tell Jipona the news.

Fatima School in the Wahgi Valley was growing year by year. When Brother Tim arrived in the Highlands, he found barren grassland stretching from the hills to the river, its only inhabitants bush rats and mosquitoes. With his partners from Australia, New Zealand and Holland, Brother Tim rolled up his sleeves and set to work to drain the swamp, burn off the kunai grass and build the school. They cut down trees and sawed their own planks and posts for the buildings. They made roads and fences, and planted the coffee bushes whose red berries brought in the money that kept Fatima School going. Now more than three hundred pupils of all ages between five and twenty-five attended the school. The original buildings had been scorched by the dry seasons and soaked by the wet, and were falling apart at the seams. Only last week Michael Kunjil, sitting at his table in the classroom, had leaned against the wall and gone head over heels backwards into the garden, taking a large section of the woven wall with him.

The boys of Fatima School came from twenty different villages in a fifty mile radius. Most of the older ones were boarders, who slept in long corrugated tin dormitories on wooden shelf beds. The younger children like Joseph walked in to their daily lessons from the villages nearby. Brother Tim had said that new classrooms must be built; but where was the money to come from? He had launched an appeal among the students. There were seven Kopi Nokpa boys at Fatima School, and they had chosen Joseph to put forward the request to the Council through Kian Kombuk.

Seventy kinas! Jipona thought about it, and sighed for the bolt of kingfisher-blue cloth she had earmarked in Rima's trade-store. Rima was too canny a businessman to give even his wife something for nothing. Cut up carefully, that bolt of cloth would yield skirts for Jipona and her sisters and aunts to wear when sing-sing was held later that year.

Rima, who had come up from the little store on the Highlands Highway for his midday meal, jabbed open the lid of a tin of Madang Tuna fish.

"When are they going to build this classroom?" he asked Joseph.

"Brother Tim said it would be before the rainy season. We're going to make a sing-sing."

Rima spoke as he spooned out a glutinous portion of canned fish into each tin bowl. "That's when the

Tambos will be here. They could come down and dance at the school with our people. They'll have everything with them — it's a pity to waste the opportunity."

Joseph jumped impulsively up, his brown eyes glowing.

"Oh, that would be . . . do you think they would, father?"

Rima chuckled grimly. "When they're here as our guests? I don't think the Tambos will say no to Berom Kibunke!"

The Tambo clan lived about fifteen miles from Kopi village, in the Jimi River valley beyond the mountain range to the north. In days gone by the two clans had been deadly enemies, and any Tambo finding himself on Kopi Nokpa territory could expect an arrow between the ribs from the first person he met. But before the white men had arrived in the Highlands, two strong big-men had come to power at the same time in the two clans, and had ended the state of war. Now there were Tambo girls married to Kopi Nokpa men, and Kopi girls living in Tambo village. Every year a great sing-sing or dancing feast was held at one or other of the two villages, partly for the elders to exchange boasts and presents, and partly to strengthen the ties between the clans by fixing up marriages between willing partners. There was a good chance that Joseph and many of his friends would one day marry Tambo girls. In fact Kopi Council had spent part of the morning's session discussing that particular side of the forthcoming sing-sing. Kian Kombuk, who had come into the house and was dipping a cob of sweetcorn into the mush of tinned tuna, looked up.

"Kibunke was saying that we'll have to be very careful this year. I don't need to tell you who will be casting his eyes on that pretty daughter of Kibunke's . . . what's her name? . . . yes, young Awala."

"Pius Pop?" Rima said with a frown. "*Ai!* I remember two years ago when that little scamp came here. He caused more trouble than a whole fighting party of the old Tambos would have done. Do you remember how he spoiled the dancing with all that row with his good-for-nothing friends? And the time he set fire to the fences in the gardens? Eh! I don't think young Raphael Kibunke will be too pleased to see him again. It was all we could do last time to keep them from each other's throat."

"I know it," sighed Kian. "I got Master Pop by himself before the Tambos went home and I gave him something to remember us by."

"Awala was very taken with him, the silly girl," observed Rima.

Kian moodily poked the fire with a kindling stick. "Yes — and now they are all nearly grown up . . . and Raphael has got very jealous of his family honour all of a sudden. Berom is worried about what will happen when Raphael and that young hot-head Pius Pop catch sight of each other . . . you know what these Tambos are like . . . "

The old man could remember the days when the very mention of the Tambos was enough to fire the blood of a Kopi Nokpa warrior. He had never quite learned to trust the former enemies.

Joseph scraped a forefinger round his bowl and licked off the last scraps of fish. Pius Pop might bring trouble with him — but that was two months away. In the meantime there was the sing-sing at the school to think about. On Monday he could tell Brother Tim that the Kopis and the Tambos would be joining forces for the celebration, and he could put seventy kinas into the big tin box that served Fatima School for a bank.

That night Kian Kombuk told one of the stories about the famous trickster of the tribe, Samboli. No-one knew whether this rogue had ever really played his pranks around Kopi village, or whether he had grown from stories told round the fire to set the listeners laughing.

"Eh! Samboli! Come here, everyone!" chuckled Rima as the old man settled himself and began his automatic rolling of black tobacco leaf and newspaper. Shadowy figures left their own fires and squeezed into the hut, while latecomers squatted round the doorway and looked in, arms around knees. Kian, sensing an appreciative audience, wetted his throat with a long swallow of South Pacific lager before beginning the tale.

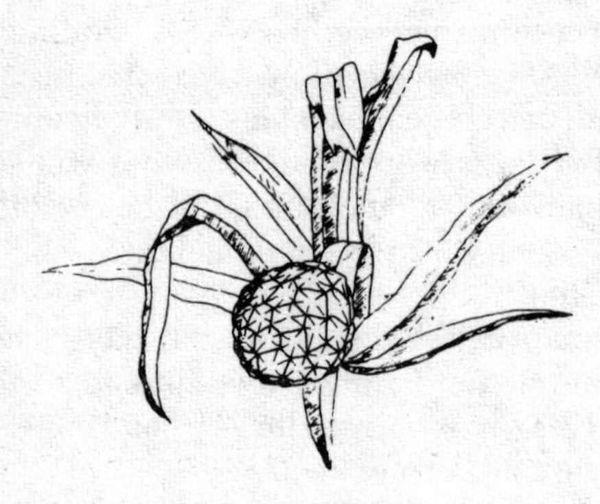

In the days when the Highlands Highway was no more than a dusty bush path beside the Wahgi, and no Tambo dared show his face around Kopi village, there were two houses for all the clan. On one side of the clearing stood the men's house, a long thatched building with a great fireplace in the centre and a low doorway. The men slept in a separate room, divided off from the main area by a six-foot wall of woven bamboo. High up under the sooty thatch were rafters of wood which ran the whole length of the house: rafters that helped Samboli to play the cleverest trick of his life.

On the other side of the clearing was the house where the women and young children slept and ate. The pigs belonging to the clan lived in this house, in a snug chamber lined with grass. Thunderer, Big-Belly and Tiny — each pig had a name, and to their owners they were the sweetest little darlings in the world. Perhaps the women who lived day and night with the little darlings had other ideas — but they kept such thoughts to themselves. The best small and tender kau-kaus were put aside and boiled up for the pigs' dinners, and on wet, windy nights it was not the pigs who went without warm grass beds in the long house.

The smallest, weakest, ugliest runt in all the herd belonged to Samboli. That pig had no name — Samboli said the extra weight would surely break its back. No tasty tit-bits or dry grass beds came its way; Samboli alone among the men had no wife, and the little beast had to fend for itself, stealing scraps from under the noses of the bigger pigs with quite as much cheek as its master and scampering off into the bush to eat them in the hollow tree trunk where it slept. The other men laughed till the tears ran down their faces whenever someone mentioned Samboli's pig. They rubbed their stomachs and licked their lips as feast day drew near, and squeezed the fat ribs of their own pampered animals, anticipating the juicy slabs of meat from the mu-mu ovens. But Samboli paid no heed. He smiled to himself, and murmured, "I'll eat all your pigs before you get one mouthful of mine."

This made them laugh all the more.

Each night the men of the village came back from the women's house to sleep. They expected a good hot fire to be blazing when they returned; and Samboli, having no wife, was always the one detailed to gather the sticks and make the fire. The men didn't like his tricks and jokes, but they all agreed he was a champion fire-maker. Every time Samboli asked for some help in gathering the firewood, the others just laughed at him.

"Help you, Samboli? No — we're too busy. Why not ask that pig of yours? He might be a little runt, but he's good for a twig or two!"

Samboli smiled and did not reply, but all the while a cunning revenge was taking shape in his mind.

As the men were going out of the house one morning, Degemba the hunter turned in the doorway. "Mind there's a good fire tonight," he told Samboli, who was scratching himself and yawning by the embers of last night's blaze. "There'll be a frost if I know anything about it."

"That won't do the poor fellow's cough much good," muttered Samboli, half to himself.

"What fellow?" asked Degemba. "No-one's had a cough for ages."

Samboli shrugged. "Oh, just the fellow who was coughing in the sleeping-room when I came in to light the fire last night. I thought it was one of you."

"Someone in the sleeping-room?" scoffed Degemba. He tapped his forehead. "You're crazy, Samboli. We were all over at the women's house as usual. No-one was here."

"Are you sure? Well, someone was in there all right — I heard him coughing away. He was whistling, too. That's odd."

Samboli shook his head and turned away, seemingly losing interest in the mysterious intruder. Degemba wrinkled his brows and ran after the others.

"Hey, boys! Who sneaked back to the house before the rest yesterday evening?"

"No-one!"

"Not me!"

"What are you talking about, man?"

Degemba repeated Samboli's story. The men looked at each other. Coughing and whistling? Who could it have been? Kunjil spoke up.

"Perhaps it was a . . . "

A breath of fear stole through the group. Degemba finished the sentence whose meaning they had all grasped.

" . . . a spirit?"

Everyone knew that the spirits of the ancestors lived up on the mountain tops. What if one of them had decided to pay a visit to Kopi village? Then strong Et the snake-killer laughed scornfully.

"A spirit? Nonsense! It's just that Samboli again with his crack-brained ideas. Why would they come down here and bother us?"

Everyone smiled. In the warm, friendly sunlight their fears evaporated as they thought of foolish Samboli and his idiotic notions. Spirits in the sleeping-room? Ridiculous! Talking and laughing with relief, the hunting party climbed on up the stony track towards the haunts of the wild pigs.

Standing at the door of the hut, Samboli watched them disappear among the trees and grinned maliciously. The seeds of doubt had been cleverly sown, and the harvest would be reaped tonight.

Night had fallen. From the women's house came

laughter and loud singing. The hunters had returned from the high bush with two large wild pigs, a boar and a sow; and many were the boastful verses chanted by those with blood on their spears.

In the forest a few hundred yards from the village, Samboli crept from tree to tree, running his hands along the tough, rope-like bush vines that hung from the branches. He was looking for one of just the right length . . . Soon he found what he wanted, a straight vine with no kinks or weak places. He hacked off the necessary length with his stone axe, coiled the vine round his arm and ran back to the dark, deserted men's house.

Samboli rubbed the vine in the soot and ashes of the cold fire-place until it was black. Then he went out again and gathered the sticks for the fire. He built up the usual pyramid of wood inside the fire-stones. Then with great care he looped one end of the bush vine round the sticks and pulled it tight. The sticks were now lashed together into a bundle; but an unsuspecting man coming into the dark house from outside would see only the normal heap of firewood in its accustomed place. Samboli took the other end of the vine, invisible in its coat of soot, and stretched up to pass it over the rafter above the fire-place. He walked across the long hut, threading the vine over each rafter in turn until it crossed the bamboo wall of the sleeping-room. He inspected the scene carefully and nodded to himself. It all looked quite natural. The free end of the vine dangled down inside the sleeping-room from the rafter above the dividing wall. He gave it an experimental tug, peering through the gloom, and saw the bundle of sticks twitch in the fireplace. Satisfied, Samboli sat down behind the bamboo partition with the end of the vine in his hand, his head poking out through the doorway, and settled down to wait for the fun to start.

At last the singing and cheering over in the women's house died down and Degemba appeared in the doorway, silhouetted by the light of the fire behind him. He had killed the boar in a full-blooded charge, and was full of pride. He gazed across the clearing and saw that the fire in the men's house had not been lit.

"Samboli! Eh, Samboli, you rat! Where's my fire? Brrrr! It's cold tonight!"

The other men came out of the women's house and gathered round Degemba. The frosty night air cleared their muddled heads, and more than one began to think of Samboli's strange tale of the unaccountable noises in the sleeping-room. They shuffled uncertainly in front of the doorway, unwilling to be the first to cross the dark clearing and go into the men's house.

"Samboli! Where are you?" called Degemba again.

"Well, I'll go and make the cursed fire," snapped Et. He strode firmly across the village square, followed by the rest of the men. Et bent down and looked into the men's house. All seemed in order. The sticks for the fire stood in the fire-place, neatly piled and ready to burn, but of Samboli there was no sign.

"Come on, boys, let's go in," cried Et confidently. "That fool's gone off somewhere. Let's get that fire burning and we can go to sleep."

He took the bamboo whip and stick from their place by the wall, crouched down by the fire-stones and began to saw sparks onto the heap of bark shavings that lay ready. The men nudged each other in the doorway. One by one they crept into the house, timid Kunjil at the back.

Et held up a flaming piece of bark and pushed it down among the pile of fire sticks. They caught and

crackled, and bright flames flickered up. Then, before the horrified eyes of the men, the whole fire, burning fiercely, left the fireplace and rose steadily to the roof of the house. A loud burst of coughing and whistling came from the sleeping-room. Et jumped up and made a dash for the door, cannoning into Degemba and knocking him flat on his way out. Men fled through the bush in all directions, shouting out, "Spirits! Spirits!" Kunjil was at the top of the tallest tree he could find, holding on with one hand and hiding his eyes with the other.

The women and children, sleepily making ready for bed, heard the faint cries of "Spirits!" and the crashing of bodies in the undergrowth. With one accord they screamed and joined the stampede. Within a few seconds Kopi village was empty, while the trees around held a jabbering multitude. Tree kangaroos and birds, disturbed by the panic, added their contributions. In the sleeping-room, Samboli rolled on the floor, laughing till his sides ached.

At last people began to venture back to the clearing. Even worse things might be waiting for them out there in the blackness. The cheerful glow of a burning torch met them as they peered nervously into the square.

"What's up? Why are you all climbing trees?" enquired Samboli innocently. "Is it a night hunt? Can I come too?"

Now it is odd that no-one asked himself where Samboli had been all this while. But the evil spirit had driven all other thoughts out of every head. Degemba seized Samboli by the arm.

"There's a devil in the sleeping-room! We heard it cough and whistle, just like you said."

"*Ai!* The fire . . . did you see it fly up all by itself?" quavered Kunjil.

"A devil? In the sleeping-room?" Samboli calmly said. He yawned enormously. "Oh, well — I told you so. Still — who believes in evil spirits? I don't, personally. Look, I've made you a nice fire."

He pointed in at the door of the men's house, where a warm fire could be seen smoking on the fire place.

"I'm for bed. Coming?" said Samboli, and went in.

"Not on your life," declared Degemba. "I shan't go in there tonight. *Aieee!* That Samboli — he's a cool fellow!"

After a miserable night huddled together on the frost-rimed earth of the clearing, the men held a meeting. All the clan's pigs must be killed at once, as an offering to the spirit. Only the smell of roasting pig-flesh was sweet enough to appease an angry ancestor.

The prize pigs were tugged from their cosy sty and slaughtered in the clearing a week before their time. Soon the delicious fragrance of roasted pork was drifting among the trees. Children swallowed the saliva that filled their mouths; any small fingers that strayed towards the piles of brown, bubbling meat were slapped away. No-one but the spirit could enjoy those delicacies now. The slabs of cooked pig-meat were heaped on leaves and carried by the wailing villagers into the bush, to be laid among the rocks at the top of the mountain.

Samboli watched the killing and cooking with his arms folded, imperturbably smiling. When the men came for his own pig, he shook his head.

"But you must, Samboli! The spirit won't go away otherwise!"

"I think he will," Samboli grinned. "I don't believe in him, you see — and neither does my pig!"

Samboli's stick-gathering expeditions led him far

afield that week. He was not seen in the village from morning until night, when he would reappear looking pleased with himself. At the end of the week Et and Degemba climbed up to the rocks on the mountain peak, and reported that the spirit had taken all the meat and left a mighty heap of bones. The sacrifice had evidently pleased him, for no more coughing or whistling was heard in the sleeping-room, and Samboli had no trouble with flying fires.

When feast-day came around, Samboli brought his lean pig to the clearing, and all the Kopi Nokpa clan gathered round in hopes of scraps from the killing. But Samboli only scratched the runt's back with a charred fire-stick and murmured, "He's too small to make a decent mouthful — and that spirit's had all the rest, eh?"

And he rubbed his stomach, licked his lips and smiled quietly down at the little pig.

HOW THE SEA WAS MADE

THE NEW CLASSROOMS WERE nearing completion. Each morning as Joseph rounded the bend in the long earth road that linked Fatima School to the Highlands Highway he could see the brown and white backs of the mission workmen and the Brothers, bent over their hammering and sawing. Kapul, the head carpenter, and his men climbed like tree kangaroos among the wooden ribs of the building, fixing beams and joists in place with hammer blows that thudded through the trees. Brother Tim and his men were racing against time; once the rainy season had begun the ground would be flooded every few hours and work would cease.

After morning lessons the boys tumbled out of the rickety old huts that were soon to be pulled down, and raced across the grass to watch the work. Joseph's seventy kinas had joined a steady trickle of money, brought in greasy, tattered notes and old fish-tins full of coins from villages all round the Wahgi Valley. Those whose clans had contributed to the building looked on the new classrooms as their own private property, and took up positions near the front of the crowd from which they bombarded the workers with much unwanted advice. Only the tolling of the dinner bell broke up the daily gathering round the skeleton rooms.

In Kopi village preparations for the sing-sing with the Tambos were well under way. Two new buildings were going up here as well, to accommodate the guests during their week-long stay. No sounds of rasping saws or thumping hammers were heard in Kopi; these huts were of wooden poles, lashed together with bush vines to form a framework on which were tied the walls of plaited bamboo and the thatched roof of Kunai grass. They were long and low; one for the Tambo women, and one for the men. The fattest pigs had been marked out for slaughter and were fed every day by the small children with choice kau-kaus until they could hardly stand on their legs. The men had dug mu-mu pits in the ground, where the pig-meat would be laid on hot stones and covered with green leaves to bake for a day before the feasting. Birds of Paradise were brought in from their mountain refuges and stripped of the long blue-black and orange tail feathers for head-dresses. The bargaining grew hot between those with feathers to sell and those with none to wear. In Rima's little trade-store the back room was half-full of waxed cardboard boxes of South Pacific beer, stacked three high along the walls. He had also done a roaring trade in red and blue bolts of cloth.

An air of excitement and anticipation hung round Kopi village; and Joseph, plunging daily from one hive of activity into the other, had his knuckles rapped more than once by Brother Mike for day-dreaming in his lessons. His own cassowary would be added to the feast, and although he was not old enough to join the dancing Berom Kibunke had placed him in charge of the water. The dancing men, gyrating in chanting lines and beating out the rhythm on their wooden kundu drums for hours at a stretch in the full heat of the sun, had to be kept constantly supplied with water which they drank from three-foot lengths of sugar-cane stem. Joseph was to see that empty tubes were quickly refilled and properly stoppered with wooden plugs to keep out the dust raised by the dancing feet. The position of water-boy at a sing-sing was an important one, and Joseph basked in his glory.

One Tuesday morning Joseph arrived at school to find the last sheet of corrugated iron being hammered on to the last classroom roof beams. Five complete buildings stood in a row under the trees, gleaming in the sunlight.

"Hello, Joe! Come and have a look inside."

Michael Tipuka waved to Joseph from a crowd of boys round the door of their own new classroom. They went inside, the hard bare soles of their feet echoing on the pink shaven planks of the floor. There was a smell of sawn wood and fresh paint. Brother Tim was kneeling by the window, screwing a shelf with a sigh of satisfaction a bamboo tube of smoking tobacco replaced it.

"Move up, you men! Here, Kian Kombuk, come and sit by the fire. What a feast you are giving us! Is this your son?"

"My grandson," laughed Kian.

"Ai! You are no chicken any more, my friend!"

Agaba Obarip, the Tambo chief, cleared a space for the old man and the boy, and looked round.

"Now then! Tambo honour is at stake. Who'll tell a tale to stretch the ears of our friends here? Where is Rul?"

"Rul! John Rul! He's back here."

A Tambo grandfather, grizzled and grinning, was pushed forward.

"Keep quiet! Quiet, back there!"

A rowdy band of singers was hushed, and the blinking story-teller settled himself on the log and cleared his throat. The fire-light flickered across his lined face as he nodded slowly across at Kian.

"Well, Kian Kombuk," he growled, "I'll do my best. You know all the stories worth telling from round these parts, so I'll tell you one I heard years ago when I used to work down at Madang on the tuna boats. Man! those were rough days. We'd sail out for ten days at a time through all kinds of weather, and we used to spend the first couple of days after each trip washing the salt out of our eyes. I could tell you a few tales about the hurricanes . . . "

The eyes of the old man looked far beyond the circle of listeners as he saw the leaping grey waves, and heard the demented shriek of a tropical gale in the rigging of a storm-tossed fishing boat. He shook his head and smiled at Kian and Joseph.

"However — I heard this story from a man from the

Trobriand Islands who had come to Madang to get work. It's a story of the sea, and a strange one . . ."

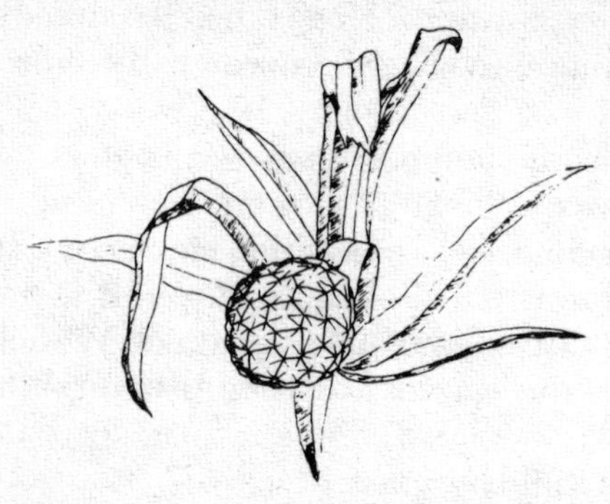

In those days, there was no sea. North, south, east and west from Papua New Guinea stretched an endless plain of sand. Here and there humps of rock stuck up above the desert, covered in trees and watered by streams, where the inhabitants lived as best they might. One day these outcrops would be the islands all the world knows — New Britain and New Ireland, Manus and Bougainville — and the Trobriand Islands themselves.

Kilao was an old, old woman. Her skin was as wrinkled as a passion fruit, and she had long forgotten the last of her many husbands. Her children and grandchildren were dead and gone, but Kilao lived on. At the very top of the highest mountain peak in all the Trobriand outcrop she had built her hut, and there she lived alone. She had no pigs and no food garden. The strength had left her arms, and she gathered fruit and roots from the jungle to help keep her ancient bones alive.

A tiny spring bubbled out of the rocks beside Kilao's hut, and every day she would hobble from her doorway to fill a coconut shell with water. Some days the spring ran low and the old woman had to go thirsty. When Kilao had been a young maiden she had not lacked for water or food; her husbands had provided her with all that she needed. But nowadays her thirst sat heavily on her, and when a sudden drought struck the mountains she was brought near to death.

One afternoon Kilao lay panting in her hut, licking her cracked lips with a swollen tongue. The spring had been dry for three days, and the coconut shell was nearly empty. She gazed at the sunlit square of the doorway and wondered if she would be with her ancestors that night.

Something rustled outside. As the old woman stared at the door, a scaly head poked into the hut. Two bright eyes regarded the wrinkled figure on the mat. Cautiously, inch by inch, a fat blue snake slithered into the room. From nose to tail he measured at least twenty feet and the coils of his body nearly filled the little hut. His mouth was open, and his forked tongue flickered over his lips. Like Kilao, he was desperately thirsty. He stared at the old woman until he was sure that she would not attack him, and then looked round the room. He saw the dull glint of the couple of inches of water in the coconut shell beside the mat and licked his lips again. Kilao was too exhausted to utter a sound. The blue snake wriggled over to the shell and draped his neck over the rim. Still the human made no move. Satisfied, he lowered his head to the water and drank until the shell was dry. Then he swallowed contentedly and spoke.

"Thank you for the water."

Kilao was too old to be surprised at anything. "You are welcome," she croaked. "Now I will surely die; but my time has come anyway. May the water give

you the strength to find more."

The blue snake seemed to smile. "Your time has not yet come, old woman. Do not give up hope. You have given me the last of your water, and now I will make you a gift in return."

He shuffled across the floor and laid his head close to Kilao's ear. "Listen, old one. Take your knife and cut off my tail. Wrap it in a leaf and bury it in the ground near the dry spring. Then you will see what you will see."

"I have never hurt any living thing," Kilao replied faintly. "Why should I cut your beautiful body?"

Again the snake smiled at the old woman. "Don't worry, grandmother; everything will be all right. Do as I say and you will never lack water again."

Kilao stared at the snake a moment longer and then got to her hands and knees. She was too weak to use her knife, but the snake himself placed the end of his tail across the blade while she held the handle. The tail writhed, and a piece as long as Kilao's arm dropped to the floor. There was no blood and the snake seemed to feel no pain. Gasping with the effort, Kilao dragged the tail out of the hut and wrapped it in a large leaf from a bush beside the dry spring. She scraped a hole in the earth, dropped the tail in and pushed back the loose soil on top of the bundle. Then she collapsed and lay still.

Some hours later, Kilao was roused by the sound of running water. She lifted her head and looked around. Night had fallen and stars were out above the mountain peak. The snake had disappeared. Where she had buried the severed tail, a pool of water was creeping across the parched earth. The old woman scrambled clear and sat down by her hut, watching the water until it ceased to spread and lay quietly under the trees, the surface gently rippling in the night breeze. Kilao crawled forward and touched the cool water with her fingers, then scooped up a handful and tasted it. It was fresh and delicious.

Kilao drank until she could drink no more. Then she filled her coconut shell, and felt strong enough to totter into the bush in search of food.

For the next few days Kilao lay beside the pool, drinking and feeling her strength return. Soon she was able to go far into the forest; and one day she walked right down the mountain to the shore of the sand sea and feasted on coconuts under the palm trees. The aches and pains left her old bones and she began to run and jump like a young girl. Something strange was happening to her appearance too; when she looked into the clear waters of the magic pool she saw the lines and wrinkles of her face beginning to disappear. Her pinched cheeks filled out, and her scraggy neck became firm and smooth once more. The snow white of her hair turned to grey, then to rich glossy brown. Kilao understood then the gift that the snake had given her; and was glad.

One day a young man from a village at the foot of the mountain made his way up the bush track to Kilao's hut. The people of the village had heard tell of the ancient woman who lived all by herself on top of the mountain, and had decided to send an ambassador in search of spells that might break the drought. The young man approached the tumbledown house with some trepidation. A woman as old as Kilao might well be in league with terrible spirits, and he was weak with thirst and the fatigue of the long, hot climb from his village.

As he pushed aside the last of the forest branches and looked up at the rocky peak of the mountain, he was astonished to see a beautiful young woman sitting by a sparkling pool of water, waving to him. The young man blinked, then stumbled forward up the path.

"Hallo, young fellow! What do you want?" asked the girl, smiling dazzlingly at the weary youth. "Um . . . er . . . I'm looking for the old woman, Kilao," he stammered. Yes — she really was lovely. Who could she be? The old woman's grand-daughter? But no-one had mentioned anything about her.

"I am Kilao," replied the young woman. She laughed delightedly as the man's jaw dropped. "Don't you believe me?"

"Kilao? But how . . . where . . . ?"

"Why don't you have a drink? You look hot and tired. Come — there's plenty in the pool," smiled Kilao. The young man gaped at her and bent down to drink, first glancing warily around as if half expecting a trick. After he had eaten the fruit that Kilao offered he explained his mission, breaking off every now and then to shake his head and stare at the beautiful girl.

"I . . . I was expecting . . . " he muttered.

" . . . an old witch?" Kilao finished for him. "Well, I really am Kilao. Don't you think the mountain air suits me?" and she held his hand flirtatiously against her cheek, enjoying his amazement.

The young man soon made up his mind that a trick was being played on him. He searched all over the mountain top for the old woman, but no-one was there except for him and the beautiful girl.

Now this youngster had a wound in his leg, an old mosquito bite that had gone bad and was swollen and sore. That night, after he had drunk again from the pool and made his bed of branches under the trees, he noticed that the wound had stopped itching. Taking a flaming stick from his fire, he held it close to his leg and inspected the injury. There was no doubt about it — before his eyes the swelling was subsiding, and an old sore on his arm was also vanishing. The young man was no fool, and he soon put two and two together. He knelt by the pool and scooped out some water which he trickled onto a scratch on his wrist. As he watched, the red edges of the scratch became smooth and brown. Within a few minutes the whole blemish had gone, leaving healthy skin.

Now he thought about it, he felt marvellous too, all over; yet before touching that water he had been as tired and sickly as all the thirsting natives of his village. It must be a magic pool; and the same power that had healed his wounds so quickly must also be making Kilao so lovely and youthful.

What a wonderful find! The young man pondered. There seemed little point in taking a few skins of water down the mountain to his village — such a small amount would only be wasted. And yet . . . the big-men must be shown the wonderful powers of the magic pool. They would not credit his tale without some pretty convincing proof.

"If the water can't come to the village," murmured the young man, "then the village must come to the water. Eh! I will take a sample, and they will *have* to believe me."

He knelt down again and drank his fill. Then he dipped into the water the old coconut shell which Kilao had left beside the pool, and carried it stealthily to the edge of the forest. Here he tied it round with several layers of leaf and tipped it experimentally upside down. Not a drop spilled. The young man took a final look at the pool and the dark hut where Kilao lay sleeping. Then he set off at a loping run down the forest path, carrying the precious shell of water in the crook of his arm.

The big-men of the clan were most indignant when the young man boldly called a village meeting as soon as he appeared from the jungle. They scoffed when he told his tale. But they had to believe the evidence of their eyes when he poured a stream of the magic water onto Umba's hand where three fingers had been amputated in mourning for her father — and those fingers actually grew out of the stumps as they watched.

After that there was no more argument. No witch, however powerful, had the right to keep such a marvellous power to herself. The big-men issued orders for the village to be evacuated. Possessions were bundled together, and the houses burned to the ground. The pigs were driven in from the bush and rounded up. Such crops as had survived the drought were carefully disinterred and packed in leaf bundles, moistened with a few drops of the magic water. The ill and lame were placed on bush-vine stretchers. By the end of the second day the villagers were on the march, winding in a chattering, excited column up the jungle track towards the peak.

Kilao heard them coming. As the barking of dogs and babble of voices rose out of the jungle, she sighed with the wisdom of her many, many years. Let them come — she could not stop them. Soon they would find out . . .

The young man headed the column of villagers, bursting with pride. The chief himself had called him "the saviour of our clan"! He was the first to run to the pool and scoop up a shell of water, which he presented with a flourish to the chief as the old man came hobbling up.

"Drink, father! Drink and be young!"

Soon the aged chief was prancing over the rocks with flowers in his hair, while the lame and sick turned somersaults and shouted with joy. The magic pool had something for everyone — even Oraki, known for his bad temper and quick fists throughout the clan, went round slapping people on the back and roaring with laughter. A happy madness seemed to have taken the villagers and shaken them out of their senses. No-one saw the beautiful girl in the shadows of the trees, crying bitterly as she watched the leaping, laughing people round the pool. In Kilao's spirit the sense of loss trembled and ached like an arrow-wound. In her hair the first streaks of grey were already starting to re-appear, and the velvet skin of her cheeks held once again the tracery of wrinkles.

All that day and the next the villagers cavorted round the magic pool. By evening on the second day the water was muddy and foul to the taste. The green grass round the edge had been trampled flat, and a group of youths was dragging one of their number towards the water. Their laughter held an ugly note, and they were making free with switches of bamboo on the back and legs of their victim. The chief was shouting at his wife to bring him food, but he had lost his authority along with his white hair and could not make her obey.

In the shallows of the pool the lame men and women paddled; but they, too, were complaining angrily.

"My leg is no better! I could bend it last night, but look at it now!"

"Stop whining, you old hag! These jungle sores are

worse than ever. What has happened to the magic water?"

"It isn't working! It isn't working!"

A child drank from his cupped hands and instantly spat out the water with a howl of disgust.

"Ugh! It tastes of salt!"

The group of youths had brought their captive to the edge of the pool. It was the young man himself. His eyes were wide with fear and bewilderment as he stared past the angry faces of his antagonists towards the discontented villagers. What had gone wrong? The breath of his captors panted on his cheek, and their eyes were hot and cruel.

"You and your stupid fairy tales! This water is worse than useless," snarled the leader of the gang. He jabbed a finger at his own thigh, where a pink sore lay open and bleeding. "It went away last night, and I thought I'd been cured!"

The other villagers, attracted by the furious voice, began to gather round the group by the pool. Other voices rose, twisted with rage and disappointment.

"Yes . . . what about my eyes? . . . my cough? . . . I thought I was young again . . . "

The gang leader snorted. "In with him . . . let him drink his own filthy water and see if it's magic enough to save him!"

"No! It's not my fault . . . I can't swim . . . " gasped the young man. He began to shriek, "Kilao! Kilao!"

"There *is* no Kilao — it's all a trick," snapped the chief. A fine dusting of grey was creeping over the black curls of his hair and beard. "This is the work of an evil spirit. He's to blame — yes, throw him in!"

The gang tripped the young man up and seized him by the wrists and ankles. The earth and sky lurched crazily round as he was swung backwards.

"Stop!"

An ancient, withered crone stood between the executioners and the pool. She glared at the villagers. No-one moved.

"You fools! You blind, idiot fools! I am Kilao, and you have ruined my beautiful pool with your greed. The magic is gone!"

One skinny arm reached out and the crooked fingers closed around the handle of the chief's bush-knife, protruding from his belt. The old hag pulled the knife from the unresisting chief and cackled, "Go back to your aches and pains, to your quarrels and fights! This magic was too good for such as you. But I will make you another gift, simpletons! I will give you more water than you have ever dreamed about. But you will not drink this water! You will make canoes and sail its calm face — you will take fish from its depths for your bellies. But the mighty ocean will only be sleeping! One day, men and women, you will know your master!"

The spellbound villagers whimpered as Kilao's voice beat in their ears.

"When the great wave hangs in the sky and your bones turn to water as you look - when your boat is tossed like a stick and the wind drives you away from the shore — when the shark circles and circles, and you are alone and weak — when your houses and your children are dragged away and swallowed one by one . . . then your master will call you to account!"

The chief's bush-knife rose above the old woman's head, and flashed downwards. It split the bank of the pool, and the old woman vanished into the earth. With a hiss as if a snake were buried underground the water spurted forward, dashing the villagers to left and right, and roared down the mountain. It reached the bottom of the slope and surged outwards, driving forward across the sandy waste in each direction until blue waves tossed as far as the eye could see. And as the terrified people on the mountain top took to their heels, they heard above the noise of tumbling water and crashing trees a thin voice that cried triumphantly, "Run! Run away, fools! But when your master calls you — there will be no escaping then!"

HOW THE FIRST MAN GOT HIMSELF A WIFE

HA!

A double column of trotting men pounded into the village square at Kopi. Their brown bodies glistened with a coating of pig-grease that reflected sunlight on the curves of muscle. Each man held in front of his naked chest a flat board of wood, decorated with crimson powder, in the middle of which glinted the golden crescent of a large kina shell.

Wai-wai-wai-wai-HA!

With a flourish the red boards were laid in two parallel rows each side of the square beside the trussed and furiously squealing pigs, bunches of prized head-dress feathers, long poles studded with pierced coins and kina notes and waxed cardboard crates of South Pacific beer. The panting men stood rigidly to attention in their two ranks, facing each other across the space of beaten earth. On each head nodded long plumes — black, white and blue tail feathers of the Bird of Paradise, brown speckled owl feathers, green and red parrot wings. The faces were fierce masks of paint. The patterns of scarlet and blue on nose, cheek and forehead had taken many anxious hours to accomplish. Round some necks bobbed necklaces of shells and pig tusks; from others hung the scraped and pressed tail skins of tree kangaroos. A thick belt made from a ring of tree bark encircled each waist. A bunch of tanget leaves covered the dancers' buttocks, and a lap-lap of hammered and woven bark brushed the ground in front of their bare toes. Fingers gripped the tubular wooden kundu drums with their snakeskin heads. The sour stench of rancid pig-grease mingled with the sweat of the men.

Hai-hai!

A gift from the people of Tambo to the Kopi Nokpa people!

Ha!

The square was ringed by an excited crowd who let out an appreciative roar as the red boards with their golden shells were laid beside the other offerings. Since the days when they were rare enough in the mountain regions to be used as a form of money, kina shells had become the Highlanders' most treasured ornament. When the Australian dollar had disappeared after independence the new Papua New Guinean money was reckoned in "kinas". The Prime Minister himself had worn a kina shell as a compliment when he had visited Wabag a few years back. Now here were fifty at least. *Aieee!* The Tambos were good wantoks!

At the top corner of the square were the Tambos who would not be dancing — women, children and the old folk. The younger women were dressed like their Kopi counterparts in bright blue and red cotton skirts. Some of their faces were painted: there were young men from the Kopi Nokpa clan to be won. The old men gossiped with the Kopi councillors, and from his post at the front of the crowd Joseph could see Kian's grey head thrown back in laughter as he listened to a Tambo tale.

Along one side were the Kopi women. In the front row the beautiful Awala watched Pius Pop as he stood opposite her, smiling fiercely through his red and yellow paint. There was a smile on Awala's face, too, but it was not in answer to the challenge of the grin of Pius. One of the black-and-blue feathers from his head-dress had come loose and was dangling comically over his face, tapping him on the nose with every breath he took. Pius would not lift an arm to replace the feather; instead he blew savagely upwards each time the blue tip came into view, still grinning fiendishly at Awala — and causing her smile to broaden.

Lining the opposite side of the square were the men of Kopi, watching the Tambo dancers critically. In the tightly-packed ranks Raphael Kibunke could not see, from his position behind him, the ludicrous feather that was tickling Pius's nose. He saw only that his sister Awala appeared to be smiling at his arch-enemy. He clenched his fists and muttered under his breath.

Then the dancing began. Round and round, up and down shuffled the lines of dancers, plumes nodding, right hands thudding out the hypnotic beat on the kundu drums' snakeskin heads. Sweat ran in streams over their grease-smeared bodies as they hopped - right foot, left foot, right foot, left foot. Hoarse chanting rose and was carried by the breeze far and wide over the forest.

With a final shout the first dance came to an end and Joseph darted forward with one of his carefully filled and stoppered tubes of water. David Mali had been chosen to help him, and he, too, offered a water-tube to a Tambo man. The thirsty dancer lifted the open end of the tube to his mouth and drank lustily. His throat pulsed as the cool stream water washed away the dust. He belched and passed the tube to his neighbour.

"Well done, boy — just what we needed."

A new chant was heard, and the Tambo dancer picked up his drum and stepped into line. Joseph and David slipped quickly out of the square and lay down at the front of the crowd. Joseph blinked, chin on hands. The hot sun burned down, the drummers' palms beat out the rhythm and the dusty feet rose and fell, rose and fell . . .

"Wake up! Wake up, Joseph! Your father is thirsty. Eh, Joseph!"

Jipona was stooping over him, shaking his shoulder. Joseph sprang up, rubbing his eyes. A blue-faced devil with a drum was beckoning to him from the dancing arena.

"Come on, sleepyhead — we're dying of thirst out here!"

Joseph gaped. The square was full of Kopi dancers, panting and dusty. The familiar faces of the village men were strange and frightening behind the masks of blue paint.

"Come on," called Rima again.

Joseph picked up a water-tube and took it to his

father. He must have been asleep for a long time. The last thing he remembered was watching Pius Pop in the centre of a wheeling line of Tambo dancers, leaping up and down and thrusting out his chest every time he came opposite Awala. David Mali had already exhausted his supply of water-tubes and had disappeared in the direction of the stream to replenish them. Joseph ran back to the edge of the square and looked around. Only one dancer had taken no water —Raphael Kibunke, who was sulking at the end of his line with frowning brow and folded arms.

The Tambo men looked on as the Kopis went through their dances. As the stubby green bottles of beer circulated their comments became more enthusiastic, and the older men agreed that although it took a Tambo to display the art of dancing at its best, these Kopis were certainly learning. But a group of youths around Pius Pop continued to pass unkind remarks. The more beer that flowed down their throats, the unkinder the remarks became. Raphael was their main target as he gyrated in successive dances. His eyes glittered angrily but he had to dance on, his blue face-paint hiding the fury that was building inside him. Now Pius was whispering to his henchman, a gangling youth with a scarred cheek named Pamben. As Joseph watched, the two of them left the group of Tambo lads and walked out of sight behind the houses.

The dance ended, and Joseph stood up. He stared after them and frowned. The great feast was due to take place tomorrow night when the pride of each clan would be at its height. Would it pass off peacefully? Or would a spark of anger touch off a real confrontation between Raphael and Pius and their followers? And would that spark ignite long-buried prejudices in the older men, to some of whom the present state of friendship between Kopis and Tambos had never quite replaced the traditional antagonism? With Pius Pop around, one could never be sure how things would turn out.

"Here, Joseph — what's bitten you? Come on; catch hold of one of these!"

David Mali was standing in front of him, a fresh load of dripping water tubes over his shoulder. Joseph shook off his gloomy thoughts, took a tube and carried it out to the waiting dancers.

"A strange story we heard last night," old Kian rumbled at the Tambo fireside that evening, "very strange. But here is one even stranger — and it goes back even further . . . "

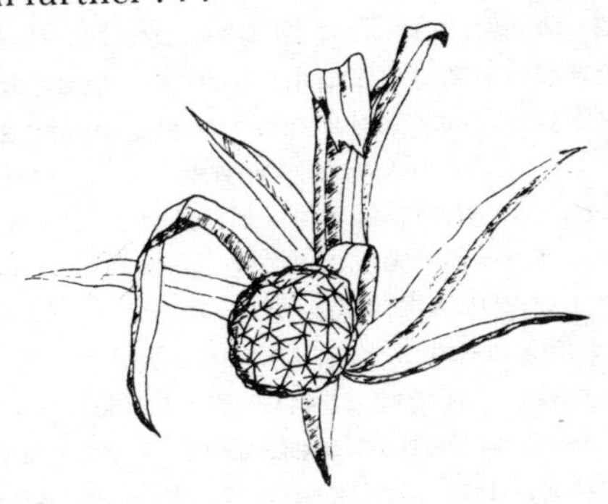

In those far-off days the sands of the coast lay untrodden by human feet, and no paddles dug the waters of mighty Sepik. The Bird of Paradise flew unmolested among the mountains of Wabag, and at night no fires blazed in Kopi. All the world was ignorant of man — save one small clearing in the deepest part of the bush. Here stood a little bamboo house, built by two brothers — Akekane and Kumankane, the very first men in the world.

It was a hard and lonely life for the brothers. There was no fire to warm and cheer them; many years were to pass before Yakes the dog would bring the blazing stick home to Womkama village and gladden the hearts of the Highland folk. There were no stories to tell, for Akekane and Kumankane each knew the other's tales by heart. Worst of all, there was no wife for the brothers — no wife, no children and no tribe.

One day it happened to be Akekane's turn to go into the bush to look for food.

"Try and bring back some pandanus nuts if you can," said Kumankane as he began to clear out the house. "We can keep them in the shells for a few days, and I won't have to go out again so soon."

"Lazy devil," grunted Akekane as he took his woven food-bag and set out into the trackless forest.

Many hours later he found himself in a part of the bush he had never penetrated before. During the long walk from the house he had grubbed up a few handfuls of roots to put in the bag, but there had been no fruit on the trees. Now he was sitting by a tiny stream that tinkled among the stones of its winding bed, resting his tired feet. Gazing across the stream, his eyes fell on a pandanus tree in the shadows of the forest. Large clusters of nuts were hanging among its spiky leaves. Akekane jumped up delightedly and splashed across the stream. Nimbly he shinned up the trunk and inspected the nuts, which were just turning from green to brown. The meat inside the husks was sweet and chewy. Akekane settled himself comfortably at the top of the tree and began to eat, flicking the broken fragments of husk in a wide circle all round the trunk. When he had taken the edge off his hunger, he opened the neck of the woven bag and picked nuts to take home to Kumankane.

All of a sudden an extraordinary thing happened. Clear across the stream came the sound of a voice, calling and laughing.

"Kumankane!" thought Akekane. "Why has he followed me?" But as he listened, he knew that this sweet, high music did not come from the gruff throat of his brother.

"What kind of animal makes a noise like that?" frowned Akekane, staring across the glade into the forest. The next moment he nearly fell out of his tree. The leaves parted and out jumped a young woman, looking back over her shoulder and laughing. Then she darted down towards the stream, while a second girl came running after her from the trees. They chased through the grass and along the bank of the stream, shouting and giggling. The one in the lead stooped and caught up some water in her hands which she hurled in a sparkling shower over her pursuer. Then both girls flung themselves down on the bank, panting hard.

Akekane's eyes and mouth were wide open as he clung to his perch and stared down at the young women. He trembled with fear till the pandanus leaves shook all round him. What were these strange yet familiar creatures? They were playing and joking with each other just as he and Kumankane did. But what clear, bird-like voices! What slim arms and glowing skins! Should he call out? Or would they run away and be lost for ever?

The girl who had first appeared now got up, still panting, and began to peer up into the trees, evidently on the lookout for nuts or berries. Her companion called something and went off into the bush on the other side of the stream. Akekane's trembling stopped, and he looked hungrily down at the upturned face of the girl. This was what had been missing from his life. She must come home with him!

Now the girl stood under the pandanus tree. She saw the bunches of nuts and braced one leg on the trunk, reaching up to pull herself into the tree. Then she saw the grinning face of Akekane among the leaves, and screamed in terror. With one lightning-swift jump Akekane swooped down to earth, arms outstretched, and grabbed her tightly round the waist. The girl shrieked out loud at the bearded face a few inches from her own, and dealt him a stinging slap across the cheek. She strained against the encircling band of his arms. Akekane held on, trying to think of soothing words.

"I don't want to hurt you! Stop struggling!" he panted. The girl cried out again, then gave a curious wriggle. A blur of colours swam before Akekane's eyes, and he found a full-grown snake writhing and lashing in his arms. The thick green body slithered through his hands and the red gleaming mouth struck its fangs into his shoulder. Blood flowed down Akekane's chest, but he gritted his teeth and held on. Magic! Well, he would not give in now.

The snake let go of his shoulder, reared up and wound its coils round his chest. Tighter and tighter they squeezed, till the breath rasped in Akekane's lungs and he sank to his knees. Now he was rolling in the water of the little stream and the snake was jerking frantically in his arms. Another whirl of colours, and he was staring into the long, mean jaws of a crocodile. Akekane ducked his head from side to side as the razor-sharp teeth clicked and snapped around his face. He clung on grimly. His belly and legs were raked by the crocodile's claws, and every few seconds the great armoured tail swept round and whacked his back and shoulders.

At last the reptile's struggles began to slacken. Akekane shifted his weight on top of the horny body, blinking away the blood that ran into his eyes. He grinned savagely.

"I've got you now! I'll drown you if you don't give up!" panted Akekane. "I want to talk to you. Turn yourself back into that creature who was under the tree."

Again came the blur of colours and Akekane found his arms empty. The crocodile was nowhere to be seen. The waters of the stream, tinted red with his blood, ran away across the stones. But scuttling quickly up the trunk of the pandanus tree was a little brown cus-cus, which stopped when it reached the top and looked down at him, chittering in triumph. A surge of fury burned through Akekane. Forgetting his wounds and exhaustion, he leaped straight across the stream and swept like a storm upwards into the tree. The cus-cus turned and with a squeak of rage launched itself into space — but too late. One of Akekane's brown hands shot out and seized a furry hind-leg. Then, holding the cus-cus upside down, he climbed back down to the ground again. He gripped the animal by the loose skin at the back of its neck and held it out at arm's length.

"Aiii!"

Akekane let out a gusting breath.

"Now I have you, little beast! Be sure I will not let you go again. Why do you not become that wonderful creature I wish to take home? I will not hurt you."

The colours flashed across his eyes once more, and there in front of him stood the young woman, smiling reluctantly and holding out her hand.

"Eh! You are a brave fighter. My magic cannot

break your grip!" She massaged the back of her neck. "And what a grip!"

Akekane reached out and touched her cheek. He found his voice.

"You and I are the same. Are there more of you?"

"Only my sister," said the girl, pointing across the stream. "We are happy together — but we have nowhere to live."

"My brother Kumankane and I have a good hut," Akekane said thoughtfully. He pondered. "But we are not happy. We need . . . we want. . . "

He looked directly at the girl. "Come home with me, and we can share what we have."

"What about my sister?" the girl asked.

"Well . . . what about my brother?" said Akekane; and looking at each other they began to laugh.

Kumankane was so surprised when he saw the two sisters coming out of the forest with Akekane that he took to his heels and ran deep into the bush. But soon his curiosity got the better of his fright, and he was laughing and swapping stories with the sister of Akekane's girl. The little hut in the clearing became a happier place from that day on, especially when the sons and daughters of Akekane and Kumankane were born. In time the new tribe spread all over the earth; and numberless are the people who owe their existence to the stout heart and strong grip of steadfast Akekane.

AMBRA MINIGA AND MR EMU

ALL THROUGH THE following day the Kopi and Tambo people feasted. Rima went out early with a party of men and brought the pigs down into the square. Each wriggling animal was held steady at its front and rear trotters by two men, while a third fitted a sharp arrow to his bow. Then the squealing pig was held up at eye-level, the bow was bent and twanged and a fresh fountain of blood splashed onto the wet, reddened earth. The carcase was gutted beside the mu-mu pits and slabs of white meat cut out and laid across the hot stones, while the village dogs snarled around the glutinous heaps of entrails. A crowd of small children watched intently, howling like fiends at each thud of arrow in hide. Jipona and the other women carried in piles of kau-kaus and pale yellow corn cobs. These were put to roast in hot ashes, while the blue smoke curled up and stung the eyes of those who sat near nursing their babies. Appetising smells drifted across the village. At last the baked chunks of pig-meat were lifted out of the mu-mu pits in a hissing cloud of steam, carefully distributed, and devoured.

At midday Berom Kibunke's truck went bouncing

down the village road to Rima's trade-store to pick up fresh supplies of beer. Songs rose and fell in the warm air, and in the background throbbed the constant beat of the kundu drums as the dancing continued.

Joseph spent most of the day plying the dancers with his water-tubes. At sunset he went down to the river, threw off his shorts and shirt and plunged into the cool water. As he floated on his back he could hear the singing, shouting, laughter and crackle of flames; and, looking towards the darkening trees around the square, he saw them swimming and rippling in the rising heat of the fires.

He clambered out and dried himself with his shirt. Then he pulled on his shorts and ran up the path behind the village. He made for the little hut in the corner of the gardens, grinning to himself in the dusk. *Ai!* Tonight his cassowary was to be added to the feast: tomorrow the Tambos and Kopi Nokpas would join forces to dance at the Fatima school celebration.

Joseph craned his neck and cautiously peeped in at the little window. Lately the cassowary had been extremely bad-tempered, and only last night had knocked the tin plate of scraps from his hand with a sharp stab of her beak as he was emptying it through the window. Now she seemed quiet enough, though — a dark shape huddled in one corner. No wonder, thought Joseph. Earlier in the day he had seen his father cut open the hut wall, grab the big bird and tie her feet together with a short rope. Rima had tumbled the heavy body into the furthest corner of the hut and quickly clapped the cut section of wall back into place, twisting a bush-vine to secure it. Now the cassowary could only walk with tiny, jerky steps, and Rima judged that she could be managed by Joseph on the path down to the village square.

Joseph felt in his shorts pocket and drew out Rima's one-dollar knife. The long blade, sharpened each day against a stone, sliced through the bush-vine that held the wall together. Gingerly Joseph eased away the bamboo matting and looked in. A faint glint of iridescence winked in the dark as the cassowary turned her head sideways to inspect the intruder, but she stayed still. The knife clicked shut and went back into Joseph's pocket, and he reached forward into the hut with a piece of string. The bird crouched motionless as he tied the string round her neck. He pulled, gently but firmly, and with a shivering of hair-like feathers the cassowary hobbled out of her prison.

Joseph wound the loose end of string round his fist until the lead was only a few inches long. Then he began to walk down the path towards the village. The cassowary seemed quite ready to come, limping after him with Rima's rope tugging at her ankles. Only a certain gleam in her eye suggested that this was no lamb going meekly to the slaughter . . .

In the village square, the hot blood of the young men was rising. Pius Pop and Pamben were sitting with their cronies, passing the green bottles of beer around and singing. Already Pius's eyes were red and his laugh was wild. The songs were made up on the spur of the moment, and most of them were about big-men's sons and the troubles that beset them. Pamben was a clever songsmith, and the Tambo youths shouted with laughter.

Nearby crouched a group of Kopi lads, with Raphael Kibunke in their midst. Too proud to defuse the situation by making a humorous contest of the insulting songs, Raphael sat with arms folded and eyes smouldering. His friends muttered and fumed as they glared across at the chanting Tambo boys. Kian Kombuk and the Kopi councillors watched anxiously. Agaba Obarip, the chief Tambo councillor, had been warned earlier by Kian and Berom about the bad feeling between the lads, but Agaba had laughed.

"I knew Pius Pop's father, old Kurai — he was a fine man! No son of Kurai's will insult his hosts and cause trouble."

Berom Kibunke, his fears a little calmed, had given Raphael a stern talking-to, and had gone off to drink beer beside the Tambo long-house further down the village. But Kian Kombuk, in the middle of his tale, looked continually across at the restless young men, and fingered a stout stick that he had been guarding all evening.

From her seat by her mother on the other side of the great fire, beautiful Awala seemed unaware of the tension centred on her. She listened attentively to the gossip of the women, chewed on a roasted cob of corn and never once glanced across at the young men.

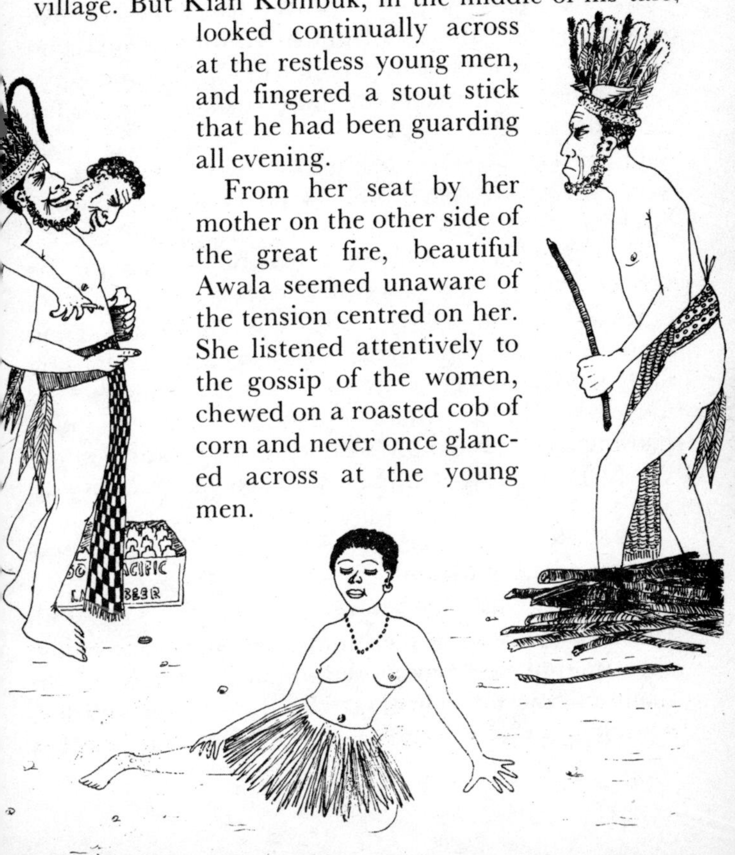

Pius Pop drained yet another South Pacific, and lurched unsteadily to his feet. He bent down and whispered in Pamben's ear. Then very slowly and with legs spaced well apart, he staggered across the square, bawling out the chorus of Pamben's latest effort.

"Tambo lads know what to do —
Not like some we know!
Tambo lads are right for you —
Not like some we know!
Not like some we knoooooooooow!"

Arriving opposite Awala, Pius stood swaying and grinning at her. Awala's head was turned away; she did not appear to have noticed Pius.

"Tambo lads are right for you —
Not like some we know!"

As the Tambo boys took up the chorus in a gleeful shout, their leader stumbled forward and brought his face close to Awala's.

"Not like one I knoooooow!" chanted Pius.

There was a cry of fury, and Raphael Kibunke jumped to his feet. All the Kopi lads followed suit. An ominous growl came from the Tambos, who were already on their feet facing their antagonists. Raphael bounded towards the stooping and leering Pius, ignoring Kian Kombuk's sharp command to stop. Slowly Pius straightened and turned to confront his enemy.

"Well, Kibunke," he grinned thickly. "What are we doing away from Mummy?"

Raphael's fists clenched and he breathed short and hard. Pius smiled insolently. The two groups of young men squared up to each other. Kian Kombuk got up and strode towards the quarrel, his grey beard jutting resolutely and his stick at the ready. Several Tambo men frowned and scrambled to their feet. Disaster was in the air.

A piercing shriek split the atmosphere like an axe. It came, not from the antagonists, but from the dark jungle beyond the circle of firelight. Everyone jumped and stared round in the direction of the noise. A rapid pattering was heard, and into the light of the fires burst like a feathered bomb the infuriated cassowary. A broken length of rope trailed from one leg. A piece of string flew from her neck behind her like a streamer. Kicking right and left, the maddened bird ran round the fire gnashing her bony beak and squawking, while the tension in Kopi village dissolved into laughter.

A tidal wave of youths flung itself joyfully into the hunt. Heading the cassowary off from escape, they drove her into a circle of bodies and closed in for the capture. But the cunning bird was not ready to submit without a fight. She slipped between a Kopi and a Tambo boy, pecking the former and clawing the latter, made for the open door of the Tambo men's long-house and shot inside. Raphael Kibunke flung himself after her with the Kopi boys hot on his heels. Not to be outdone, Pius Pop and the Tambos smashed their way clean through the bamboo wall at the far end, and confusion reigned in the dark interior. At the height of the uproar the wily old cassowary suddenly emerged from the heap of shouting, laughing bodies, dashed screeching through the shattered end wall and fled into the night.

"She knocked me over and snapped her rope," mourned Joseph.

"You be thankful she didn't give you a kick to remember her by," replied Rima. "I told you never to trust one of those brutes!" He uncapped another bottle of beer and drank deeply, then wiped his lips with the back of his hand. Kian Kombuk chuckled.

"*Ai!* I haven't laughed so much for years! It's the best thing that could have happened, Rima — just listen to those young fellows now!"

Tambo and Kopi voices rose in a ragged chorus, and roll-up cigarettes passed from hand to hand. Raphael Kibunke lay on his stomach near the fire, massaging a bruise on his arm, surrounded by a crowd of lads of both clans, roaring with laughter as Pamben and Pius launched a "cassowary hunting" song upon the air. Awala had disappeared some time ago, but none of the youths had noticed.

"Things will be all right now," murmured Kian Kombuk as he watched the cheering crowd. "Tomorrow will be a dance to remember at that school of yours — thanks to your precious cassowary! And that reminds me — pass that bottle, Rima, there's a good fellow — that reminds me of the story of old Cassowary's cousin, Mr Emu, when he gobbled poor little Ambra Miniga by mistake . . . "

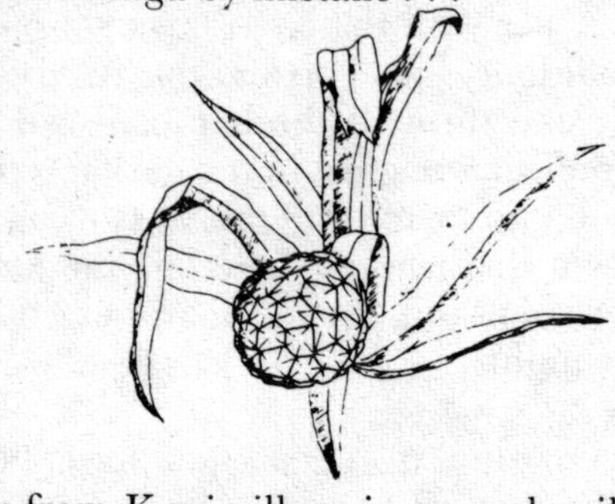

Far away from Kopi village in a much wilder part of the country is the lonely Mount Ambra. Its shaggy head rears up above the jungle, and in the early morning the clouds make a ring around its shoulders.

Birds love the quietness of the untrodden bush, and in the vicinity of Mount Ambra they can build their nests and rear their young undisturbed.

At the very top of Mount Ambra lived a plump little bird with a scarlet head and breast named Ambra Miniga. He was a chirpy fellow, always bobbing in and out of the other birds' houses. Everyone liked Ambra Miniga and his cheerful twittering song. Ambra Miniga's house was a ramshackle affair of twigs and leaves. It was getting draughty and uncomfortable, and Ambra Miniga made up his mind to build a new one. He knew he could rely on the other birds to help with the construction work, but first he had to find the bush-vines he needed for the binding of the roof and walls.

Off he flew, darting from tree to tree, testing and tugging the bush-vines that twined in the branches. None seemed quite right. Ambra Miniga fluttered on to the very thickest part of the forest. He perched on a bush and sat still, considering the building materials around him.

Pat-pat-pat! Down the path came Mr Emu Long-Neck, looking for berries. His bright eyes flicked from one bush to the next as he licked his sharp, ever-open beak. His long toes spread wide as he paced along, elegantly turning his head this way and that. Clusters of round, fat, red berries hung on the bushes, and among them sat Ambra Miniga — round, fat and red —quite still for once in his life, so intent was he on his plans for the new house.

Ambra Miniga did not see Mr Emu Long-Neck. But Mr Emu saw Ambra Miniga as he came abreast of him, and he mistook him for an exceptionally large berry. Out stretched his long neck. Snap! went the big beak. Ambra Miniga was plucked from the bush and swallowed whole. Mr Emu Long-Neck blinked at the feathery taste.

"Hmmm! Some of these berries are not over-ripe. I'd better move on and find a fresher patch," thought Mr Emu, and he stalked on down the path.

When he had eaten his fill, the sun was high in the sky and he had begun to feel a little sleepy. At the edge of the jungle was a grove of shady trees which cast a cool shadow on the ground. Soon Mr Emu Long-Neck was snoozing happily under a tree, his neck extended on the grass. Slowly his beak began to open as he snored. From the dark cavern of his mouth two indignant eyes peered out.

A bedraggled, berry-spattered little body emerged, dragged itself over the rim of the beak, fell into the grass and gasped there crossly. Mr Emu Long-Neck slept peacefully on.

It had been a most unpleasant experience for Ambra Miniga, jolting around the jungle inside Mr Emu Long-Neck, paddling up to his neck in the dark in a mass of half-digested pips and skins. Ambra Miniga staggered away to clean himself in a nearby stream.

"Really! Fancy eating me! Too stupid to tell the difference between a bird and a berry!" grumbled little Ambra Miniga as he scrubbed the fruit stains from his plumage. "I certainly shan't invite him to my house-warming party."

Back on the top of Mount Ambra, the other birds clustered round Ambra Miniga to hear the tale of his adventure and to laugh at foolish Mr Emu Long-Neck. Soon they had commenced work on the new house. The old, rotten twigs of Ambra Miniga's previous house were pulled out by many willing beaks and thrown away. New walls and a new roof were cleverly sewn together by the Weaverbird. Soon the new house was finished, and a proud little Ambra Miniga settled in — but not before he had invited all the birds of the bush to a celebration party — all the birds except Mr Emu Long-Neck.

The news spread like wildfire through the jungle, and early on the day of the party the guests started to arrive. First to appear were the parrots, who racketed noisily up from the bush and surrounded Ambra Miniga in a raucous crowd. Then they fell greedily on the piles of fruit and nuts laid ready by Ambra Miniga. Their chatter and screeching laughter advertised the start of the party. Soon a pair of white cockatoos perched in the branches to feed and swap jokes with the parrots.

A loud song broke in on the revellers, and a yellow-bellied whistler hopped from the jungle to greet Ambra Miniga.

"Whee-ee-ee! A fine new house!"

Whistler gripped a branch with his black toes and ran his sharp beak along the leaves, scooping up insects.

Next to arrive was the Honey-Eater in her red and black suit. She twirled down to the ground and bobbed a curtsey to Ambra Miniga.

"Over there, my friend," said Ambra Miniga, pointing to a rotten tree-stump covered in sweet-smelling flowers. "You can sip your nectar in peace, away from those rowdy fellows round the fruit piles!" Honey-Eater gave Ambra Miniga a grateful chirrup and busied herself among the bell-shaped flowers.

The sun rose up into the sky and the happy noise of whistling, singing and cackling filled the mountain peak. More and more birds arrived to see the new house and to meet old and new friends. The Pied Fly-

Catcher pirouetted above the gathering, winning loud applause with a dazzling display of aerobatics as he snatched midges from the air. Bower-bird brought a present — a carefully selected offering of shells and stones, all in varying shades of red in honour of Ambra Miniga. He set them in place around the new house before joining the feast.

Suddenly a shadow fell across the clearing, and all the merry-makers looked up. A chill touched every heart as the great silhouette of the King himself, the dread Mountain Eagle, circled massively downwards. Timid Honey-Eater shivered and crept inside a bell-flower as the eagle landed and folded the magnificent span of his wings. His hard orange eyes stared round at the guests. Silence reigned.

"Er . . . won't you come this way, your Majesty?" stammered Ambra Miniga, who had sensibly prepared for the possibility of a royal visit. The day before the little bird had found a freshly-killed rat abandoned by a gorged tree python, and had laboriously dragged it up the mountain. But one could never be sure of the King's temper, nor of how he might react to such a gift. At previous celebrations he had been known to prefer his host to the proffered food, and today, as always, he had dropped in uninvited and unannounced. However, after another suspicious stare all round he hopped over to the rat, sniffed it, turned his back on the other guests, and tore it to shreds. The birds hastily resumed their own conversations and titbits, not caring to look at the bloody feasting of the only meat-eater among them. Soon the King was sipping the last gobbets of rat blood from his beak. He flexed his talons and turned round to hold Ambra Miniga reflectively in his remorseless gaze. There were no words of thanks, no congratulations, no

parting pleasantries. A blur of brown feathers, a rush of wind, and the eagle was spiralling upwards into the sky as the guests let out a collective sigh of relief. Chatter broke out again more gaily than ever.

From the shadows of the forest the last guest shyly peeped forth — the gorgeous Bird of Paradise, flirting his long white and orange fountain of a tail as he stared anxiously up at the departing King. Ambra Miniga bounced up. "Come on, Paradisaea. He's gone now. Come and have some berries — I've saved some beauties for you!"

The singing and display went on. The piles of fruit and nuts were nearly gone. "A speech! A speech from Ambra Miniga!" screeched the parrots.

Ever ready to oblige, Ambra Miniga hopped up on to a low branch and faced his guests. Just then a surreptitious movement among the bushes at the back of the crowd caught his eye. A long sharp beak and a long stringy neck poked out inquisitively.

"Well, my friends, I'm glad to see you all here," began Ambra Miniga. "It has been a long time since such a gathering of our folk — not since the last great flood of the Jimi River, I think, when I seem to remember our brothers the Parrots putting on a wonderful display of singing to raise our spirits . . . "

All the guests laughed and turned around to cheer the irrepressible parrots, who chittered and cat-called cheerfully. Behind the assembly a beady eye fixed on the nearest bunch of berries, and a heavy body stole out from the cover of the leaves on long, silent toes.

"We have met here today to celebrate the building of my new house. Many kind friends have helped me, and I'm very grateful to them all. The Weaverbird has sewn the walls beautifully — I'll be snug in there for a hundred years! — and I'd like to say a special thanks to Bower-bird for the decorations."

Mr Emu Long-Neck had reached the berries and was cautiously inspecting them. Ambra Miniga carelessly snapped off a piece of branch and played with it as he went on.

"But we must not forget someone who was not asked to be with us today . . . someone very well-known to you for his frugal appetite and graceful flight . . ."

All the guests had heard Ambra Miniga's tale of his unhappy expedition. They laughed loudly, and cries of "Mr Emu Long-Neck! Where is the old misery?" came from the parrots.

" . . . but someone who has turned up anyway!" shouted little Ambra Miniga in his loudest voice, and he threw the branch with all his strength. It flew over the heads of the crowd and hit Mr Emu Long-Neck square on his back. He had just grabbed a juicy bunch of berries, and now he let out a frightful squawk. All the birds turned round. With the bunch of berries dangling from his beak the thief turned tail and dashed away down the hill. Above the laughter of the guests rose the cheeky chirrup of Ambra Miniga.

"Enjoy your berries, Mr Sticky-Beak!"

Mr Emu Long-Neck lay low for many days after the party. When he walked abroad again he found a crowd of little birds ready to follow him all day, shouting out, "Sticky-Beak! Sticky-Beak!" — and that is what the little birds still do!

SAW-SA

IT WAS THE LAST DAY of term, and school was over. Joseph was just turning off the Highlands Highway onto the Kopi track when a dusty Mercedes lorry overtook him, beeping its horn. From the passenger window waved Rima's brown arm. The lorry swung up the track to Kopi village. Its powerful engine rumbled as the driver changed gear at the bend and accelerated up the final incline into the village square. It pulled up under the trees and Rima jumped down from the passenger door.

"Hey — ya! Jipona! I'm back, woman!"

Two or three idlers stopped to watch Rima as he strode across the bare earth to his house. Hearing his voice, Jipona came out with little Piau on her arm. Joseph had run up in the wake of the truck, and now he darted across the square and hugged his father.

"Hello, son! Well, I'm back. My word, Lae is hot at this time of year!"

Rima had been down to Lae, the big city on the coast at the eastern end of the Highlands Highway, to visit his brother. On the way back he had stopped in Goroka to make arrangements for a new firm to supply his trade-store. Now he was in great form, cracking jokes with the villagers who stopped to chat.

"Where is Kian Kombuk?" Rima cried suddenly.

"Here," came a quiet voice from behind him, and Rima turned to find the old man watching him sardonically from the doorway of the house. "You're so busy talking, you haven't even set foot in your own house," chided Kian.

"Never mind that, old man," shouted Rima. "I've done a wonderful deal at Goroka — I'll be a rich man before long! And, hey — guess who's driven me up from Lae!"

Rima whistled and beckoned. The driver of the Mercedes, who had been quietly smoking and watching Rima's antics, clambered down and advanced.

"Saw-sa!" gasped Kian. "Saw-sa!"

The driver was a tall, thin old man. His face was deeply lined and one eye-socket was red and blank. Across the bridge of his nose and down one cheek ran a white scar, which disappeared from view under his chin. It would have been a nightmare face, Joseph decided, if the remaining eye had not been twinkling with fierce humour. The puckered mouth grinned widely.

"Well, Kian! It's been a long time."

The newcomer's voice grated far down in his throat, a harsh grunt which made Joseph look to his father for reassurance. But Rima was laughing delightedly as he watched the two men grasp each other by the elbows.

"Old Saw-sa, Jipona! I found him in a bar in Lae. The old devil gave me a lift in his truck — all the way up!"

"Hmmm . . . and I suppose he'll be wanting to stay? Well, he can find his own blankets."

Joseph stared at his mother in puzzlement as she turned on her heel and went back into the house without a word to the stranger. But the newcomer did not seem in the least perturbed. He and Kian were cackling away together like a couple of old hens, wiping tears of laughter from their cheeks, while a group of Kopi villagers gathered round with their mouths open. "Saw-sa! Saw-sa!" the whisper went round. Rima was listening to the old men with an appreciative smile. Joseph stooped under the kunai grass fringe of the roof and went inside.

"Who is he, mother?" he asked. "Why don't you like him?"

Jipona swung round on her haunches from the fire and looked hard at her son. "Ah, your eyes are not as blind as some other people's!" she exclaimed. Then she resumed her placing of fat kau-kaus among the glowing ashes. She did not seem inclined to go any further. With a sigh Joseph hunkered down next to her and began to sort through the pile of kau-kaus.

"That man has caused your grandfather more trouble than anyone else," Jipona suddenly said. She jabbed crossly at a burning kau-kau in the fireplace. "I won't tell you what they used to get up to — stories not fit for a boy to hear." Joseph had never heard his mother's voice so angry. "Kian Kombuk was never out of trouble when he was a lad — just like that Pius Pop. He didn't mend his ways until that man left the Highlands. My mother used to say the happiest day of her life was when she saw Kinal Parange walking down that path — and she knew he wouldn't be back! She'd been your grandfather's wife for four years by then, and she told me she didn't start to like him till Kinal Parange finally left him alone."

Joseph looked out and saw the two old men roaring with laughter. Kinal's eye glittered with mischief. He looked more like a naughty boy than a villain.

"What happened to his face?" Joseph asked over his shoulder. Jipona came behind him and grunted as she looked out at her father and his crony.

"I can't remember now . . . some foolish prank years ago . . . something about a storm down at Lae." She prodded Joseph in the ribs. "And no encouragement from you, my lad, when your grandfather gets his tobacco going tonight. We can do without the sort of tales those two will bring out between them."

Jipona sniffed. She was still very cross. "Kinal Parange's name was an evil word to my mother all her life . . . he has a lot to answer for. I wish your father could have left him where he found him!"

It appeared that Kinal Parange, or "Saw-sa" as Kian continued to call him, had business with his truck in Mount Hagen and would be driving there tomorrow morning. He intended to come back tomorrow night to sleep at Kopi village, and would drive back to Lae the following day. Jipona snorted angrily when she heard he would be spending another night in the house, but said nothing.

Joseph was fascinated by the scarred face, hollow eye-socket and enormous energy of the scrawny old man. He leaped about the village, talking and laughing nineteen to the dozen, gathering firewood, fetching water. The villagers shook their heads and murmured, "Eh! Saw-sa!" Everyone seemed to know him and hold him in affection — except Jipona. Kian Kombuk and Rima spent all that evening talking to him, chatting and swapping reminiscences while Jipona and Piau withdrew to visit friends. Joseph had not been forbidden to stay, so he sat quietly by the fire and listened with all his ears while the two old friends spoke of fights, wounds, drunken evenings and storms at sea. The atmosphere in the dark house grew thick and blue as the smoke from the fire and the black tobacco hung sluggishly below the thatch.

"And how is your brother?" Kian asked Rima at last when Saw-sa had gone out for a few minutes.

"He's very well — and he'd like this young scallywag to go and stay with him." Rima smiled at Joseph, who could hardly believe his ears. Go and stay by the sea! Now the holidays were here he would have five whole weeks to spend as he liked.

"Yes," went on Rima as he knocked the cap off another bottle of beer. "They all said they didn't see enough of us. Their house is just by the beach, and the two lads are about Joseph's age. This morning they brought me a whole green coconut with the top cut off and the sweetest milk I've ever tasted inside. I drank it after I'd had my swim in the sea. Wouldn't you like that, son?"

Just then Saw-sa came lurching back into the house, and Joseph heard no more about his invita-

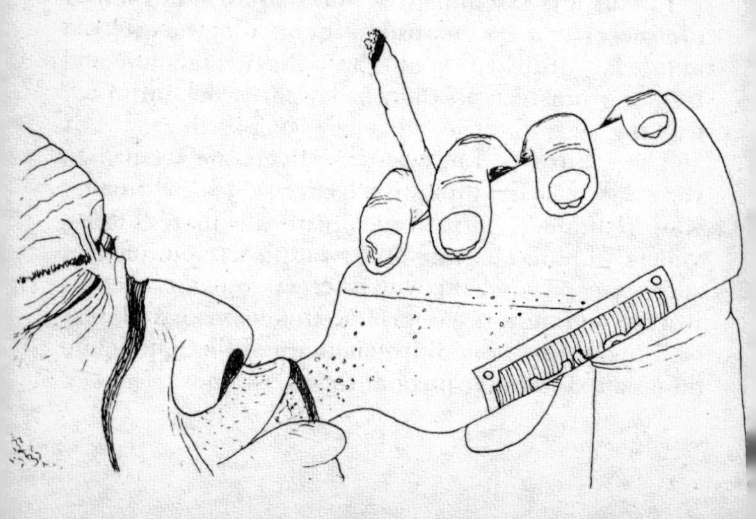

tion. But he lay awake late that night on his mat, too excited to sleep. Two cousins . . . palm trees . . . ships . . . bathing in the waves of the sea! He stared up at the thatch where the rats rustled and squeaked, until the snores of the three men lulled him to sleep.

Next morning Saw-sa was soon gone on his way to Mount Hagen, and Joseph and his grandfather were enlisted by Rima to carry the Goroka stores from the roadside where Saw-sa had dumped them into the little trade-store. The job took all morning, and Kian and Joseph took their food up at midday onto the grassy bank overlooking the Highway. At last Joseph was free to ask the question that had been burning on his tongue.

"What happened? It was a long time ago, just before your mother was born — by the way, I've an idea she doesn't care for Saw-sa. Well, he and I were down at Lae, helping with the fishing-boats, when a storm blew up: one of those hurricanes." Kian's finger corkscrewed round to imitate the twisting wind.

"We were about five miles out to sea, and we ran like lightning for the harbour. We'd just cleared the bar and were going down to our mooring when a loop of fishing net overside caught up on a big metal buoy and held us there. The wind was really screaming and the sky was green and black. I was scared out of my mind."

The gnarled fingers twisted a long leaf of tobacco as the old man looked back thirty-five years. "The water was doing this" — he wagged his hand up and down violently — "and the skipper and I got the lifeboat ready and jumped in with the two other boys who worked on the boat. We grabbed an oar each and were well away from the ship when we realised that old Saw-sa wasn't in the lifeboat with us."

Kian had looked back at the fishing-boat, and saw Kinal Parange leaning out over the bows calmly cutting the net free from the buoy. He seemed quite oblivious to the danger, and methodically continued to hack at the strands of netting. The skipper, alerted to Kinal's action by Kian's tugging at his sleeve, shouted something, but the words were whipped away and smothered by the howling wind. Then a wave crashed over the lifeboat, and in the fight to keep her afloat they lost sight of the ship. The hurricane pushed the little boat towards the shore, and the first of the great surf breakers caught them and tipped them over. Kian found himself on the sandy beach on his hands and knees, coughing up salt water, while the skipper and the other boys did the same nearby. When Kian had got his breath back, he had staggered to his feet and stared out across the harbour.

"I could just see that old boat tossing up and down like a mad thing, with Saw-sa clinging on and cutting away." The old man shook his head in admiration. "That was him all over! He just couldn't bear to see a good boat wrecked — and she would have been split up against that buoy in a few minutes. Anyway, she came free at last, and I saw him get his hands around the tiller to try and steer her round . . . hopeless, of course, in that wind. She just came straight ashore and half-way up the beach, with that fool still at the tiller!"

Kian Kombuk smiled. Joseph waited, but his grandfather had nothing more to say.

"But the scar — and his eye, grandfather! What about them?"

"Oh, the scars! Well, when the boat hit the shore the mast snapped clean off, and the broken end caught Saw-sa right across the face. We managed to get him to the little hospital they had there in those days. It was full of people who had been injured one way or another in the hurricane. The doctor stitched him up as best he could, but of course he couldn't save his eye. Do you know, the skipper was so grateful to Saw-sa for rescuing the boat that he took him on full-time when he got better. That's when he left Kopi village for good."

Kian scratched his head and frowned. "Yes — and that's when I started to use my brains a bit!"

He rolled up the rubbed leaf and set one of Rima's matches to it, and lay back, propped on one elbow, puffing clouds of fragrant smoke. Then he winked at his grandson. "And now you want to know why everyone calls him Saw-sa . . . eh?"

Joseph nodded. It was pleasant lying here on the bank, with the prospect of his holiday at Lae to mull over and his grandfather's voice rising and falling in its rich bass rumble.

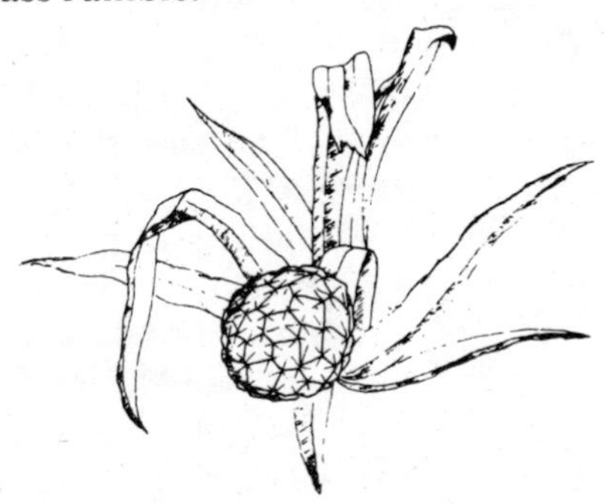

Kinal Parange and Kian Kombuk were a couple of lads in search of mischief. Like many of the other village boys in the Highlands, they were not content with the traditional life of hunting, gardening and warfare once they had come into contact with the

European explorers with their aeroplanes, their radios and their leather boots. They hung around the trade-stores and bars of Mount Hagen, a small settlement which was growing week by week. The Europeans hired them from time to time for expeditions into the bush or for general labouring, but there was never enough of this kind of steady work to occupy spirited young men like Kian and Kinal. Disenchanted with their clan life, cut off from the ideas of their parents and from the white men's life-style, they were rootless vagabonds trusted by nobody. Kian had a job with a gang keeping fires burning all day under overhangs of rock along the route of the infant Highlands Highway. Heated in this way during daylight hours, the rock was supposed to contract and shatter when the night frosts gripped it — a hit and miss idea, and Kian soon lost patience with it.

Kinal Parange at last managed to get a job driving trucks for the Leahy brothers. Kian began to make trips to Lae as soon as the road was passable, living on the beach under a crude shelter of palm fronds and turning his hand to any kind of work the fishing-boat skippers required. He already had his eye on Jipona's mother, but the bride-price was still far beyond him and a young man could not save much from fishing-boat wages, still less establish himself with the pigs and property any father-in-law would want to see.

Those were lonely days for young Kian. Kinal joined him at Lae from time to time, but his truck driving often kept him in the Highlands. During one of these times when the two friends were apart, Kinal Parange got involved in the incident which earned him his life-long nickname.

Kinal had only one redeeming feature in the eyes of the Kopi people — he was a superb grower of vegetables. His patch of garden was often neglected nowadays, but when he took some trouble the size and quality of his kau-kaus broke many a heart among his hard-working neighbours.

At last the day came when Kinal began to pay some attention to the charms of Ainno, the young daughter of one of his uncle's friends. For several weeks he kept away from the bad lads of Mount Hagen and tended his fences and garden. All of a sudden the patch of ground that had served him adequately for years was too small. Tall trees grew all round, and Kinal Parange did not care to spend several sweaty days cutting them down with a stone-bladed axe. He borrowed two dollars and set off early one morning for Mount Hagen to buy himself a saw.

Mount Hagen in those days was nothing but a street of stores and a cluster of houses. Kinal wandered in and out of the stores, scratching his head over the different items on sale — primus stoves, mosquito boots, compasses, sacks of dried vegetables. Arriving finally outside the Coltra store he looked in the window. There were long bush-knives, metal forks and spades, pocket knives and spanners, screwdrivers and chisels: but not a single saw. Nevertheless, it seemed the right kind of shop. Kinal trod gingerly over the threshold and approached the counter.

"Yes?"

The smart young assistant in white shorts and shirt had himself been a village lad only two weeks before, but by no more than the curve of his raised eyebrows he managed to suggest the gulf that lay between him and his customers. Kinal scratched his scalp and looked sideways along the shelves.

"Yes? What do you want?"

The assistant leaned both hands on the counter and

stared at Kinal, who fidgeted uneasily. He had seen the gangs at work on the roads using saws to cut down the trees that stood in their way. But now he suddenly realised he had never heard the word they used for the tool. He had the image of the thing clear in his mind, but how was he going to explain it to this superior young man with the patronising smile and the impatiently tapping fingertips?

"I want . . . one of those . . . "

The assistant waited, clicking his tongue loudly, as Kinal used his hands to mime the saw's to-and-fro action.

"Those things with many teeth."

The young man reached back behind himself without taking his eyes from Kinal and unhooked a large garden fork from its nail on the wall. He laid it on the counter, and laid his own hand beside it, palm up.

"One dollar fifty."

Kinal unhappily looked at the fork.

"No."

The assistant sighed. Kinal looked along the shelves behind the counter. No saws anywhere. Again he moved his hands backwards and forwards, causing a group of men nearby to turn and stare at him.

"I want . . . one of those things that bite the trees."

Very deliberately the assistant stepped over to another shelf and brought a heavy bush-knife back to the counter. He unsheathed the blue steel blade and made a pantomime of extreme sharpness by running his thumb along the blade and jerking it away with a violent hiss of breath.

"Here. Three dollars. Very good."

Again the pink palm was laid flat. Rima squirmed. He pushed the bush-knife and the fork away and banged a clenched fist on the counter.

"No! Idiot! I don't want those!"

The young man sniffed. He fetched a spade and offered it to Kinal with a contemptuous smile.

"Fool! Stupid green parrot!"

The assistant ground his teeth. He was losing face. No village *kanaka* should speak like that to a man of business. He was uncomfortably aware of the interest the other customers were taking in the scene.

"That thing with the sharp fangs! . . . You know — the one you push backwards and forwards!" shouted Kinal, beginning to sweat. A band of men from Kopi village had just entered the store, and recognising Kinal they pushed their way up to the counter to see what was going on. A burst of laughter accompanied Kinal's vigorous gestures, and the assistant stalked off to find the manager.

"What do you want, Kinal? . . . oh, one of those . . . yes, I've seen the white men using them . . . don't know what they're called, though . . . anyone know?" The Kopi men gathered round Kinal in a shouting, gesticulating bunch, each man offering his own advice. Here came the manager, a stringy Australian in a sweat-stained shirt.

"What's up?"

"I want . . . the brother of the axe," said Kinal. "I am making a new garden."

The Australian was new to Mount Hagen and had not properly learned pidgin English. He understood only the word "axe", and was offended when the shiny ten-dollar specimen he brought out was knocked furiously from his hands.

"Hey! What'd you do that for, sport?"

A large crowd had gathered outside the Coltra store by now, and men and women were delightedly watching the interplay through the window. They cheered and hooted when the Australian waved crossly at them to go away.

"Listen, cus-cus brain!" — the Kopis inside the store howled with glee — "I want that thing you push backwards and forwards!" Kinal was enjoying himself now as he sensed the audience. He violently rocked his entire frame to and fro, miming the cutting of tree-trunks. His elbow caught the edge of a display stand and sent nails and screws showering over the floor. The Kopis doubled up.

"Oh, God!" groaned the manager. "You clumsy galah!" He grabbed Kinal by the arm and made to push him towards the door. Suddenly Kinal had an idea. What was that sound they made?

"Saw-sa! Saw-sa! Saw-sa!" he hissed in the Australian's ear.

Saw! The manager raised a hand and motioned comprehension. He dived beneath the counter and pulled out a long cardboard box. Putting it on the wooden counter, the manager untied the string and extracted a gleaming new saw.

"Two dollars."

"That's it . . . at last!" shouted the Kopi men and carried Kinal and his saw triumphantly out of the store, leaving two crumpled dollar bills on the counter. The manager crunched after them over a carpet of nails, slammed and locked the door and with a sigh went round the back for a broom.

"Saw-sa! Saw-sa! Saw-sa!" chanted the Kopis as they paraded down the road to Kopi village. And ever after, the spare frame of Kinal Parange has been greeted by the nickname that celebrates his adventure of forty years ago . . . Saw-sa!

DOWN THE HIGHWAY

THAT EVENING, RIMA announced to his wife that Joseph would be going to stay with his uncle at Lae. There was no reason, he said, why the boy should not travel down with Saw-sa in his truck the next day. Saw-sa could drop him at his uncle's house and pick him up again in three weeks' time, when he was due to make another run to Mount Hagen.

Saw-sa nodded, his bright eye twinkling. He seemed quite happy to fall in with Rima's plan; but Jipona frowned. Clearly she did not like the idea of entrusting her son to a stranger, and especially not to Kinal Parange. Then she caught sight of Joseph's anxious face watching for her reaction. Joseph knew quite well that it was Rima who would make the final decision; but he did not want to upset his mother.

"Well . . . " Jipona hesitated. "If Kinal Parange is willing, and will drive carefully . . . "

"Of course he'll drive carefully, woman," Rima interrupted, rolling up his eyes.

"Don't worry, Jipona," Saw-sa told her. He held out his hands. "Look — steady as a rock. I've been driving trucks on the Highlands Highway since they made it."

Kian Kombuk nodded. "Yes . . . Saw-sa drove for the Leahy brothers back in the old days before you were born, Jipona. He knows what he's doing when it comes to handling a truck."

Jipona had more faith in her father than in the impetuous Rima. She shrugged and resigned herself to the inevitable. Rima produced a roll of dirty old notes from his pocket and counted out twenty-five. He paused, thinking, and added five more to the bundle.

"Put these in that bag, boy. Look after it carefully, now - everything's expensive in Lae, you know!"

Joseph woke shivering under his blanket. A thick white mist had rolled down from the mountains in the night, and droplets of water covered the wooden frame of the doorway. He crept out and blew some life into the dormant ashes of the fire, crouching well down and keeping out the cold with arms locked crosswise around his neck and over his chest — the Highlands overcoat. He was halfway inside his shirt when his awakening thoughts fixed themselves on the great event of this very day. Lae!

"Up, Joseph? Let's have some food."

Joseph's head emerged like a rat from a hole, and he looked across the room at Saw-sa, up on one elbow and grinning at him. Soon the two of them were squatting by the fire, alternately yawning and taking bites of cold kau-kau. Rima and the old man were still fast asleep in one corner. Near their humped forms lay Jipona, beginning to stir, with baby Piau's small head just visible between her shoulder and the top of the blanket.

Saw-sa went out to check his lorry and its load. Joseph stood in the doorway and watched him tugging at the cords that braced the green tarpaulin over the

pile of boxes and sacks on the trailer. He smiled and linked his fingers, stretching out his arms in front of his chest and yawning again. *Ai!* Lae tonight! Why wouldn't his parents wake up?

By the time the sun had shredded away the morning mist Rima's household was astir. Jipona packed some cold food and the precious bag of paper money into a small string bag, and Joseph wriggled with impatience as Rima gave Saw-sa detailed instructions about the route to his brother's house.

"Don't worry, Rima," smiled Saw-sa. "I'll see he gets there in one piece. Are you ready, young fellow? Right — jump in. Kian, my friend — take care of yourself. We're not quite as young as we were!"

Jipona reached up into the lorry's cab with a parting present from Rima's trade-store, a yellow baseball cap with a long peak.

"Behave yourself, Joseph. Don't give your uncle any trouble! Don't forget your lunch in the bag." She turned to Saw-sa. "And just you look after him properly, Kinal Parange!"

"All right, all right," muttered Saw-sa.

Joseph settled the new cap on his curly hair and hugged little Piau when Jipona lifted her up.

"Da-da-de!" gurgled the baby, and tried to grab the peak of the cap in her fat fist. Joseph handed her down, and gripped the seat between his knees as Saw-sa climbed in, banged his door and started the engine.

"Goodbye, father! Goodbye, mother!"

The long snout of the 6,000 c.c. Mercedes nosed down the track away from Kopi village. Joseph leaned far out of his window.

"Goodbye, grandfather!"

He saw Kian Kombuk raise his right hand and shout, but the farewell was lost in the throaty roar of the engine. Then a cloud of swirling dust blotted out the little party in Kopi village square. Joseph looked back until the bend in the track shut away the village. Then he sat forward on the edge of his seat and gazed through the windscreen at the sunny mountains of the Wahgi valley, coming up to meet him.

Author's Note

I collected these stories while I was working as a teacher for the Voluntary Service Overseas organisation in Papua New Guinea at Fatima High School, Banz, in the Western Highlands District. The students who gave me the stories came from several different tribes in the Highlands, each with its own separate tradition of story-telling. I have mixed together stories, names and locations in order to give a general picture of the life of a small boy in the Highlands of Papua New Guinea, alternating as it does between the modern-day world and the stone-age village culture.

I would particularly like to thank these students (now all grown men) who contributed stories to the collection: Arnold Umba for 'How Fire Came to the Highlands; Michael Maso for 'How Lai and Ambum Joined the Sepik'; Philip Num for 'Why Cassowaries Don't Fly'; Pius Umbu for 'Samboli Plays a Trick'; Kaipel Siwi for 'How the First Man Got Himself a Wife'; Michael Jiting for 'Ambra Miniga and Mr Emu'; Arnold Papa for 'Saw-Sa'; and an anonymous contributor for 'How the Sea Was Made'.

I am also indebted to Father Peter van Adrichem and Brother Kevin Laws of Fatima High School, and the other Australian, New Zealand and Dutch Christian Brothers, who welcomed a green stranger into their midst and seasoned him by example so wisely and patiently.

Christopher Somerville